INFINITE ROOMS

Also by David John Griffin

The Unusual Possession of Alastair Stubb (2015)

INFINITE ROOMS

DAVID JOHN GRIFFIN

URBANE
Publications

urbanepublications.com

First published in Great Britain in 2016 by Urbane Publications Ltd
Suite 3, Brown Europe House, 33/34 Gleamingwood Drive,
Chatham, Kent ME5 8RZ
Copyright @ David John Griffin, 2016

A CIP catalogue record for this book is available from the British Library.

ISBN 978-1-910692-60-8
EPUB 978-1-910692-61-5
MOBI 978-1-910692-62-2

Cover design, text design & typeset by David John Griffin

Printed and bound by CPI Group (UK) Ltd, Croydon, CR0 4YY

urbanepublications.com

MIX
Paper from
responsible sources
FSC® C013604

The publisher supports the Forest Stewardship Council (FSC®), the leading international forest-certification organisation.
This book is made from acid-free paper from an FSC®-certified provider. FSC® is the only
forest-certification scheme supported by the leading environmental organisations, including Greenpeace.

To Matthew Smith, for believing.

"The face is the mirror of the mind, and eyes without speaking confess the secrets of the heart."

Saint Jerome

"There is always some madness in love. But there is also always some reason in madness."

Friedrich Nietzsche

"All that we see or seem is but a dream within a dream."

Edgar Allan Poe

1

Crouching naked inside this cocoon. I clutch my knees like an ancient astronaut and although wrapped in darkness, live in mindrooms of detail and clarity. You, Dr Leibkov, continue to exist at the periphery of the solid mental landscape.

Look, over there, fishermen hosing down wooden slats, the moon's brightness making them glow. Don't know if you're still unable to see. Let me describe it for you anyway. Over by a bench, under one of the lights, a knife sharpener touches an oilstone. He's engraining oil in whorls on his thumb. Huddled spectators blink at the wind. I guess even pretenders get cold.

Here she is, my bewitching Bernadette, glowing more than anything. Drawn to her always. I'm part of her, hypnotized by her beauty. There might be a proper introduction another time.

'Let's hold your hand,' she says. Watch her gaze at me with love from those mystical eyes of hers, if you can.

When will it start?

A wailing horn emanating from a ship, ebony rectangle cut

from the mist, avoiding floodlights from the quay. Growling from a generator. Chains, powdered with rust, becoming taut in the gloom.

'Hear that?' Bernadette says. 'Not long.' And this difficult watery birth begins.

Flukes emerge first, as tall as I stand, the body rising from the waves. Those chains keep on dragging, glistening tons of flesh heaved onto the slats. A harpoon protrudes from the beast, gouging the planks. Butchers sharpen their knives – hear the hissing steel.

Time stolen to display the slaughtered one with clamour and commotion; rattling and creaking until the wind quietens and the generator stops. This whale is streaked with barnacles, longer than a train carriage, an impressive bank of blue-grey flesh.

I'm drawn to visit the mammal. It shouldn't be here under these stars. Its place is the empire of the deep, surging within a sapphire ocean. And here I am, standing by the wall of it. I'll pluck one of the filtering bones lining the jaws. So pliable I almost expect a harp-like tone. Stroke inside the furred mouth; run my hand over its smooth leathery skin. Step back to the side.

A coarse-faced fisherman climbs a stepladder and raises his knife. Plump moon flashes phosphorous in the blade. It's a signal. There are more knife-wielders appearing from out of the shadows into the yellow and silver. They lacerate the creature around the head with their oilskins squeaking. They make the deepest of cuts.

Bernadette is breathy, chilled. I'll stand behind and bring her to me. She pulls the sides of my overcoat around her. Overwhelmed with her warmth. A pulsing bliss. She belongs to me. I smell shampoo mixed with those stronger alien odours fouling the atmosphere.

Surely I only imagine the whale breathing, traumatized and seeing.

More chains slithering like tentacles. Hooks at their ends embedded about that slit. The ocean is sending fingers of foam racing up the slats, rushing and whooshing, never reaching. Shuttered moments of silence and inactivity. Sounds from the drumming waves are sounds of my breathing. I might become the ocean for a while. Can you at least try to view that wardrobe standing in the surf as if watching, doctor?

The generator groans into life again. Chains jerk. Thick skin ripping away from the slitted head, exposing blubber. The underside of the skin looks like pith of an orange. Clouds of reeking steam rise into the fogged night. No pause for mourning or remorse as cleavers hack and knives plunge into the sides of this peeled animal. Nothing can stop them. They're cutting sizeable chunks of red meat, laying them on a platform as though building blocks for some gruesome, nightmare igloo.

This place in my vision skips like missing video frames: already onlookers are haggling. Wives crowd about the scales clutching wicker baskets to their sides, eager to buy the meat.

Seagulls have ventured into the night. They spin in the dark. Hot rivulets of blood from the carcass, streaming to the ocean.

Bloody sinew, bloody muscle, bloody bone.

What more do they want? You've made me bleed.

Make Aaron bleed? No, couldn't bear the sight. Dismantle him but without the wrenching, without blood. Rotting vegetable matter, that'll do. I buried him in the deepest of mindrooms behind a furnace barrier. He did something terrible, dreadful. Perhaps he was responsible for harpooning the whale.

'What do you think?' Bernadette calling, her bright face looking out from the wardrobe. Don't know why she's there but at least safe in the cocoon. Please come out next to me then I promise I'll tell. And protect you more, you know I will.

What do I think on this occasion? Saddened because of the slaughter marring our honeymoon. This is what spoilt it. I think many things, frightening or tedious things, sometimes those with no picture, without substance. The most worrying are memories that are somehow not part of me, as though created by a type of enemy.

Listening aren't you, Dr Leibkov. I understand you're still blinded to the mindrooms. At the moment you're no more than a cerebral embryo. Hear this: when created to my satisfaction, selected and tailored mindrooms will replace the outside. That'll happen, trust me.

More details of the honeymoon? Definitely not. Some aspects must be private. I'm entering another mindroom anyway. Through the entrance, the iron arch of Penshart Press, into the forecourt. Herbert the gatekeeper marches out of his cabin wearing his official expression. This cabin looks more like a beach hut today with strings of pennants along its sides.

'Ah, it's you, Donald,' he says with a stylized salute. 'Back to the grind, I see.'

Must hurry. Those dull premises are calling.

'Good morning,' Sarah says in reception. 'Nice time? Mr Morris phoned yesterday—'

Before she can finish, Stones has thundered through the door from the printshop, muttering, 'See me straightaway.'

Strict and humourless business is already smudging the fading truths of my romantic vacation.

Stones' office. He's staring at the brochure which lays like an exhibit on the otherwise empty desk. A lamp spots it; the blinds are shut. His lips tight and turned white, eyes have moistened; temper saved for this moment. If only I had the courage to confess I couldn't care less. My new bride is all that's important.

Nobody else, nothing else matters.

I'll inspect the brochure with a hard stare, give a fair impression of concentrated scrutiny. But I shouldn't be here. I need to be at home with my Bernadette.

'Waiting, Clement.'

Did you speak, doctor? Just a disembodied voice, possibly originating from over by the water cooler.

Sudden comprehension has jolted. There, at the bottom of the brochure, a word of the slogan is misspelt. How, when I pride myself on impeccable proofreading?

'I'm sure I instructed Wally to read that before I went away.'

A weak excuse, I realize. I'll amend it this very second. There: perfect spelling.

'Donald, you ol' rascal. Seems like months you've been abroad.' Freddie talking, muffled by the clamour of printing machines, those intricate mechanisms as big as whales. 'Good time, know what I mean?' He's nudged me with an elbow. 'Changed the sheets every day, did they?' His cackle is lost below the sea of sound.

I'll smile to let coiled tension evaporate, have it drawn out by the honest clanking roar of the presses. They seem to be printing on paving slabs. The wardrobe appears to be hovering.

'I'd better get on.'

Freddie nodding but I don't think he caught it. I'll have to raise my voice.

Bernadette patting me on the chest. 'Why are you shouting? Don't get worked up, silly.'

'Yes, sorry; turmoil of the day.' I can still hear a distant rumble of machinery. This mindroom is quieter though. I'll merge with this dream woman, us as one entity; touch her again, encompass her. I sense her colours. I'm compelled to kiss while I slide one of my hands to the middle of her back then further still.

'Oh no you don't.' She's pulling my exploring fingers away. 'I'm busy with the dinner.'

There she is wandering into the kitchen like a delicious fantasy.

'Elephant grass growing in the garden.' A pertinent remark as I peer through these French windows. 'I'll get the mower out.' Grasses and rushes – even foil-covered panels – obscure anything else, like a gate or tree, or an outside existence. I'm not completely certain this is home.

Bernadette pushing open the doors of the serving hatch, her face still glowing with magical auras, moonstruck. 'Dinner's ready.' She's extending a arm then playfully pulling me to her. I'll pretend to climb through the hatch into the kitchen which is warm and aromatic from the cooking. She's planted a kiss on my forehead. An enraptured shudder has engulfed me. Doctor, how I adore her, how my fresh lady needs me! I have an urge to trill like a canary.

'Leave the garden,' she says. 'We'll do it after we've eaten.'

'You are saucy, I meant the grass.'

'So did I.' There's her mock pout.

'You do know by the time dinner's finished I might not feel like doing it.' My sly grin, continuing the game.

Bernadette is laughing. One of those light, vibrant laughs which tinkles about us. Listening still, doctor? She's next to me, speaking quietly as though others were in the room,

'Afterwards then.' A sparkle in those hazel eyes. We embrace and I feel her close, actually touching. I can, I really can.

Scene one. Woman moves on stage right, smooths tablecloth, serves steaming vegetables from dishes to already-seated man. Man leaps up, 'Nearly forgot.' Produces bottle of red wine and corkscrew; putt goes the cork. Close up, camera three, we want those strings of effervescence in the wine glasses. Pull back, wider screen, whole stage; zoom in once more to muted conversation. Discreet actions, private signs, the whole shrouded with vignette. No, not the cheap cotton wool love, none of those hazy shimmerings. Good, now we have it – firm yet refined love, soft enough to wallow in, able to repel invaders, be a womb, a refuge.

Scene two. Every frame of excitement to be captured. On the stairs, another intimate movement of the hands. 'Not even eight o'clock, naughty.'

At the portal. Soundman, let's hear rattling of the handle – give me a sensuous rattle – the squeaking hinges as a friend. That laughter, it must possess eternity and hold the spa of rapture, have joyous echoes and live on until we fade to black.

You're leaning back with a creak of seat leather, the notebook resting on your knee. I can see you quite clearly, Dr Leibkov. Your chair is next to the wardrobe, both being pummelled by the dark waves.

Still you misunderstand. It's perfectly obvious, now I've

decided. My wife Bernadette doesn't exist yet in the outside world. She never has. Simply a figment of my extraordinary imagination. I mean, if there's no evidence of a human presence, how can we say they ever existed in the first place? I just dreamt of burning photographs.

Can you read a person? I've the ability to strip away layers to discover true crux of character. You ought to have this faculty, being a shrink.

We show only a small part of ourselves. The majority is hidden below the surface like an iceberg.

I'll tell you a secret: I possess urn-shaped thoughts on plinths. Others less used are under glass. A few required at rare times are kept in beds of sawdust, nailed up inside crates. That's where Bernadette's fictional persona is stored, the memory of her creation buried as a souvenir. Put in a cellar, an unlit mindroom, miles underwater, sealed with sediment, possibly for protection.

So here – deep, deep in my mind – there's the perfect rendition of Bernadette waiting to be formed. The imperfect version seemingly outside of me sometime in the past was activated in a peculiar way by sparking neurons in a mass of synapses.

True fiction memory, moulded, repaired and perfected, can be future fact. And that with special time alignment can be past present. There, I've said it.

You think I'm misguided. I have to be honest, I'm beginning to be annoyed by your attitude. You seem an impostor on occasions, a person more suited to treating horses or fixing cars, not clients with headaches. Though I have faith in you remaining, I really do. Eventually you'll understand the time and reality shuffling I'll accomplish.

Bernadette hides in my special mindrooms, waiting to be brought into being. Form and cherish her perfect existence to come. Do you see? Nurture her realness from within. I alone hold that key. We will become no less than a dual soul. I'm naked to be reborn. I have instigated a rebirth for us. I've prodigious abilities to do this. Your acceptance and guidance will accelerate the process.

Though if I'm capable of imagining a wife then why not others? You, doctor, could be no more than a set of electrical potentials, a series of triggered electrons. But please, I need you to be real too; dare to say you must become a surrogate father. But how can you if you don't exist? I'm lost. Just a drifting iceberg in an empty, ice-melted ocean.

Row, row, row your boat…

After madness of the night, illumination is bringing sanity. Twilight is turning, evolving with early morning strands of light dyeing the sand. Tide has receded to leave barnacle-encrusted rock formations. Gulls are unsettled by a piece of flotsam in the water. The bobbing object could be sea-battered timber or a bottle containing an obscure message.

Haven't I shown my feelings and specially locked mindrooms enough? You've trawled an interesting catch, you must admit. And with unexpected bonuses too – my theories

I'm talking about – as sought after as the coelacanth, as rare to hear as the real dream, the becoming.

How does the wardrobe manage to balance so precisely on top of the harpoon? I know you're inside the cocoon. You must have tremendous skill to maintain that state of equilibrium. I'll jump up onto the flagging tail fin and walk along the remains of the whale, stepping from bloodied bone to bone.

I can reach out to open the wardrobe door. Now I see the interior is coagulated black, as if a black hole, swallowing you and everything else.

Perhaps you are unreal and always have been.

Wait though, Dr Leibkov, I need to ask something more before you leave.

If I'm imagining you, then who is imagining me?

2

The question trembled on Donald Clement's lips and dragged him to awareness with impatience. No vague dribbles of reality today. Eyelids flicked open, eyes focused – away from his reverie – onto the vertical slash of light at one edge of the wardrobe door. The light stood before him like a silver pole, as if a tangible object to be taken and wielded as a lance.

The next images to form: a beach with scattered oysters, starfish and semi-precious stones; pearls studding the sand, catching sunlight, looking like globules of mercury. Gulls, with beaks of bronze, hovered with lazy wings over the young woman swimming to the shore.

Clement pushed on the wardrobe door. The pole of silver thickened then was silver no longer. It became a swatch showing a sample of floorboard and rug, a strip of wallpaper, windowpanes stained with a red reflection, and a ribbon of ashen sky. Enough light ran into the wardrobe for him to inspect the clocks, one each side of him, and the matchsticks and elastic bands taped in patterns to the wardrobe's sides.

Feeling was lost to his legs, each hair on them raised higher upon a pimple of chilled flesh. He was paralysed from his cold, rigid position throughout the night. Yet although spending uncomfortable hours inside, he was unconcerned. Satisfaction with his experiment easily dismissed the discomfort. Scientists have abused their own bodies to gauge a drug, artists might endure unbearable situations to uncover buried wonders, he was certain. Resist temptations to make life easier if it would dilute results; suffer for the sake of clarifying facets of a long-forgotten science, a form of alchemy. This required focused determination. He believed he must be obsessive despite the psychiatrist's disagreement. There are many others and so few of us, he reflected.

After a decision to evacuate the cramped space he gave a count of two and leant to one side, the wardrobe door swinging open with a whine. He toppled out to collapse onto the rug, his tall frame bent into an embryonic position.

He smelled dust. A muted autumn morning was in the apartment. One of the landlady's cats had found its way into the bedroom again and was sponging a pillow with its paws. The abrupt appearance of Clement made it anchor its claws to the bed sheets. The cat had ravaged a packet of biscuits. Crumbs and biscuit splinters lay between a pillar of books and a television set, the screen of it facing a wall and covered in tin foil.

Clement began to rub his calf muscles and the base of his spine to induce life back into them. His neck had become fixed. He faced the bedside cabinet, his pyramid of unopened cartons of medication and a block of matchboxes upon it. Another clock stood on the floorboards with its crooked moustache showing twenty minutes past six.

A beautifully horrible sensation, the prickling to the flesh, washes of blood burning from the inside out, taut muscles throbbing in pulses…

What if the landlady came in and saw him curled on the floor with not even socks on his feet? Surely she would blush and enquire after his mental condition.

He reprimanded himself; he should have more confidence with his objectives. Perhaps now and then his actions might appear nonsensical or seem to verge on the ludicrous. Nevertheless, only a short while longer before he stumbled across the master key, the knowledge of how to initiate a clean start with Bernadette. That couldn't be illness in anyone's book.

He stood with difficulty to face the wall opposite the window. A good-sized canvas for daylight to apply itself in rectangles of orange, Fauvist impressions of windowpanes.

And there the kites hung, pinned to the picture rail. They were in the likeness of exotic birds.

Clement grunted with disappointment. A dream the day before had prophesied a surprising event. Both kites had gained organic substance, becoming what their shapes represented. Crying out with joy he had seen them fly into the middle of the room, rustling and crackling. He guessed that part of the cocoon experiment wouldn't have duplicated this miracle exactly but the least he had wished for was to see flapping, however weak, of plumped craft paper wings.

How many failures do I experience – he asked himself while pulling on pyjama bottoms – and how much more to endure? When might the imbued matchsticks and elastic bands of ability attain charmed properties to guide me? When would time weaving be finished to show the wondrous tapestry?

Back by the wardrobe, he checked the interior panels to see if the tin foil had become ripped. It seemed intact. Still more than enough protection from radio waves, television rays and computer webs. Those high-tech surveillance procedures which warped and corrupted mindrooms could still be blocked with the simplest of methods, he had discovered. The use of an everyday roll of foil easily defeated them. After the landlady's refusal to comply with the simplest of instructions to avoid psyche infiltration he realized it wasn't necessary for her — perhaps he was the only one being targeted by unseen agencies, those who would want him corrupted.

He scattered matchsticks and rubber bands from the base of the wardrobe onto the rug with a sweep of his hand. On impulse, he retrieved one of bands. While holding it open with a finger and thumb, another finger strummed it within a light shaft from the window. How powerful the elastic bands were with their impressive qualities, elegant in their simplicity. He spoke a mantra: 'Circle of light, orb of female earth, supreme loop without beginning, without end.'

The cat jumped from the bed. With whiskers twitching, the animal followed him into the kitchenette. Clement switched on the kettle. Although he still felt chilled, he opened the door onto the communal balcony to let fresh air into the musty rooms before stepping outside.

The sky was cyan scrubbed with charcoal. A miserable morning with the promise of rain though still with a sun creating weak shadows. His sight followed three sides of the balcony which overlooked a weed-infested courtyard until his view fell upon Mr Shanklin on the lower floor. The old man was leaning precariously over the balcony railings, straining his neck to the dull heavens. He aimed along the length of a broom, pretending to fire shots at an advertising balloon – the shade of lead – seemingly glued to a cloud.

'Morning, Mr Shanklin,' Clement shouted. The reply was an impression of a spitting gunshot. 'Won't impress me with false reality checks,' Clement muttered. 'Impress him one day; I'll walk over this yard with its derelict motorbikes and mildewed mattresses. Like a tightrope walker, only better. Wave in perfect circles, empowered by Bernadette's refreshed love. Anything will be possible.'

He was considering whether or not to throw more aluminium foil down into the courtyard. Yet another electrical device had been dumped there below him; he couldn't be too careful. But then the kettle in the kitchenette gave an energetic whistling as a call to return.

Once he had thrown a tea bag into a mug he drowned it

with water from the kettle. The bag bobbed to the rim, bleeding blackness. Then he took two rashers of bacon and an egg from the refrigerator.

The girl has reached the beach. Her hair is a glistening mat, drying like skeins of seaweed. Water beads run from shoulders down to her breasts. Sand clings in sodden clumps between her toes and lines the soles of her feet. She plunges back into the surges of salty water.

No she didn't…

This is what I like about mindrooms – he told the doctor – I can tailor a new room as required, tune it to perfection. She will skip along the dividing line of sea and shore, straying to the beach where pearls are trodden into the golden stretch of sand.

The frying egg ejected a boiling gob of fat and it stung his face. It had happened again: he had broken egg shell, freed the jelly contents into a pan, placed bacon rashers under the grill as well, without a conscious thought concerning his outer reality.

When he had been courting Bernadette in the mindroom vision, not a single moment of his journey to her house could be recalled. Which way had he walked? Did he use the underpass and if so, how had he escaped unscathed, untouched by drunks and the addicts? He would make certain that when visiting Bernadette in the real dream, he would avoid that underground tunnel.

He added milk to the tea; he lifted out the tea bag with a spoon and slapped it into a bin. A lorry droned past and rattled the panes in the lounge. He put the cooked food onto a plate. The slippery egg, and the bacon blistered and shrunken, appeared inedible. The tea had acquired greasy spots. A disc of mould floated to the surface of the hot liquid. Clement pushed away the plate and mug and went to the bathroom.

The bikinied female was bending, collecting satin spherules from oysters, placing them into a canvas bag tied by a cord about her waist. And as she farmed the molluscs with a penknife, leaving their shells and mash, wheeling gulls landed beside them. They poked the delicacies with their beaks, pulling away elastic strips.

A cliff yawned along the swathe of beach, pitted with jagged clefts and uneven with protrusions. Along its base were rock pools with crabs and shrimp living there amongst shadows and motes of sunlight. Sea kale grew in untidy patches. Higher up, clumps of stringy green sprouted. Higher up still, bushes defied gravity, their roots exposed and clinging to the cerulean rock face like mountain climbers. And at the summit, the intense shape of a man stood, looking down.

Clement brushed his teeth. He remembered his gums bleeding when he had scrubbed them with a toothbrush a few weeks before. He finished washing and found a razor to rid himself of his beard. And after hacking at his hair with scissors, he shaved his head.

He inspected himself further. A final decision had been made. 'Yes, my confirmed identity this morning,' he declared confidently. This special day deserved special clothes again, he decided. He spoke to his reflection: 'A refinement phase. Tribute to divine womanhood, higher consciousness; appreciation of tender female encapsulation.'

After Clement had removed his pyjamas he put on underwear, tights and a skirt. Make-up was applied in a clumsy way and nail varnish painted as best he could; only then did he put on a white blouse.

He took a wig from the bathroom cabinet. Before placing it over his shaved head, he adjusted the silver foil lining the inside. Clement had the idea that computer webs would be strong today. Infrared as well, ramped to an elevated frequency, trying to burn his barriers as they always did.

He returned to the kitchenette, disposed of the cold breakfast then closed the door leading to the balcony. Carrying his overcoat and a holdall – containing a change of clothes and shoes, as well as extra make-up – he went out of his apartment. He locked his main door and descended the stairs to the first floor landing with slight trepidation in his step.

Before turning to the final staircase he had a notion of the landlady's presence on the ground floor. He wanted to go back to his apartment but knew any delay would make him late.

Without warning another door creaked open. A grizzled head poked out with eight digits – chalk-white and dirty-nailed – gripping the doorframe.

'Is she there? I know she is,' Mr Shanklin said. 'Tell 'er I'm dead.'

Clement went reluctantly down the creaking staircase. When he had turned the corner he was presented with a bulk of a woman, haloed by light filtering through stained glass around the main front entrance.

'Two birds with one stone,' he heard. These words plummeted within him, joining his hopes of avoiding the landlady. The stone she had spoken of seemed to lodge in his windpipe. 'Follow me if you please, deary,' Mrs Froby continued and her weighty carcass jolted into movement.

Clement found a voice, a throaty version, not his voice at all, 'Work today, I start a new chapter. Really must dash or won't be able to consolidate the new dream. See you tonight on my joyful return. There's no trouble about the—'

'I know you're shuffling about up there, Benjamin Shanklin,' Mrs Froby called past him. 'You can't roost in your den forever or else you'll simply fade away. Remember our arrangement.' Anxious gasps from above but Clement considered it was his special imagination. 'Come with me, you dowdy bird,' the landlady said and then gave a short laugh.

Although he wanted to run out and fling himself down the street in a sprint, he found himself obeying without argument. He cursed — as well as trying to animate kites and use charms to continue the work of materializing an unspoiled Bernadette, he should have tried another configuration to avoid this gross woman.

For a person who owned such a large building, it often surprised Mrs Froby's guests that she lived in one of the smaller apartments. And it was made smaller still by an unconventional habit of stocking her rooms in duplicate. In her living room were two identical armchairs with horse-hair foaming from splits in the hide seats. Facing those were coffee tables, both littered with balls of newspaper and half-eaten chocolate bars. Grotesque jardinieres acted as sentries to portable television sets. A couple of clocks on the mantlepiece kept pace with each other and in one of the corners, a pair of radios stood. The surfaces of her sideboards were covered with papers and magazines, and both with a bamboo cage upon them, each housing a yellow-headed cockatiel. By chance, the cockatiel twins – Donimo and Beatrix – preened their pastel blue feathers at the same time, as if a mirror image of each other.

Clement gave a sweeping glance of suspicion to the televisions and radios.

Precise memory of a heated argument the day before began playing for him as clearly as if watching a film. Moment by moment, sentence by sentence, the inner reality was becoming more focused. This new mindroom began to overtake, becoming more real than anything about him…

Yesterday's photographic memories made present were dismissed by a thick utterance. 'Arthur!' the landlady yelled. Her body slumped onto one of the scruffy chairs and she picked up a picture frame holding Arthur's portrait from a coffee table. She gave a wheezing sigh. 'Blowhorn's still not home. Miss breakfast again if he's not careful. Giddy goat, he can be.'

But surely, Mrs Froby, you are the giddy goat, Clement wanted to say. Would she never accept the fact her husband had ceased to exist in this dimension? His monochrome photograph – strangely shaped moustache, pinched cheeks and lazy, drooping eyelids – only that remained.

'As you know,' the landlady began again but then interrupted herself by grabbing one of the chocolate bars. She twirled the wrapper from it. The bar was savaged, her pebble eyes finding animation as she ripped a chunk from its hard brown end. 'I wouldn't normally ask, but its Arthur, you see.' She paused to swallow the mouthful of confectionery. 'He will keep on. It's about your rent again. I've told him, give him … give her a chance. I said you might be two months overdue and we're no charity, but she needs time—' another enthusiastic bite of the chocolate bar, '—would he listen?' She sucked her top denture with a slurp, exposing the livery underside of her tongue. 'Not my Arthur.'

Clement had missed the words spoken. He had been standing at the edge of the cliff, peering down to the girl breaking open oysters and collecting pearls. And there, far away, a string of water intersected the horizon.

Then the water fountain was coming from a closer patch of sea. The gulls, with their bird intuition, had collected ranks and were flying in formation, screeching, to the cliff edge. This new audience watched the young woman beachcombing; saw a giant curve of black break the sea's surface; were silenced as another jet leaped up from it like a geyser.

The girl paused in her task. She said, 'I've the distinct impression, deary, you're not listening to me.'

Clement, who had been standing in front of Mrs Froby with his fingers linked behind his back, sat on the arm of the duplicate chair and replied, 'I have, every syllable. Beginning a new employment opportunity this morning. The agency is benign. Seems real.'

Mrs Froby was too busy with a stick of chocolate-covered nougat to reply. Clement waited, quietly and respectfully, despite becoming impatient to leave.

Whenever he spoke with the landlady he held an odd mixture of admiration and repulsion. He admired her determination, the clinging to her ideals, her obsession to duplicate household items. This showed strength of character. Surely she was one of the few. Made of bone and flesh even. Yet she would never hold full membership for she was obviously mentally disturbed.

Arthur is gone. Missed his dream return, no doubt trapped in a strict regime of boiling lakes and scarlet caverns. He's abandoned you, left you with your unreal apartments, rat-infested courtyard. Arthur is finally deceased, Mrs Froby; buried, decomposed, dissolved...

Clement was bellowing his thoughts so loudly in his mind that when the landlady fixed him with a stare, he wondered whether she had heard.

'New employment,' she was saying, 'what a wonderful pair of words. But you must understand, Arthur tells me you've said them before. Well, not wanting to take sides—' She let her sentence be unfinished with a preference to finishing the nougat.

Slices of light sat in between slats of the venetian blinds covering the window. Some of these slices were projected over the patterned wall and were fanned over the duplicated ornaments on the mantlepiece. More light runs sat over the landlady's lap, striping her ample bosom, thick lips and double chin. And with each movement of her highlighted jaw there was a double clock chime to accompany it.

'Half past seven,' said Clement. 'I'm going to be late. Got to go.' He was trotting to the door, continuing, 'Tonight Mrs Froby, it'll be sorted. Successful explanations to the doctor, I can assure you.'

Mrs Froby called after him as he rushed through the doorway to the front entrance. 'It will never do, Arthur will say. Our daughter wouldn't act irresponsibly, if we had one. Arthur will be very angry. Suitcases in the hall tonight, deary.

Arthur will pack them.'

Donald Clement was in the street. He needed an advance on his salary to solve the immediate problem. Perhaps he would see the agency the coming evening. He was certain they weren't a false dream. Then surely the landlady would pacify her imaginary husband.

Still fresh in the town, not yet polluted by car exhausts. Another half an hour before the main commuter onslaught, before fumes linked traffic-jammed cars bumper to bonnet like elephants at an old circus holding trunks to tails.

The concave mass was growing larger. The girl sang, unaware of danger, until a shadow fell and turned the beach to carbon. The whale rose from the sea and advanced upon her: it had grown four legs. Each huge foot crushed the sand, impacting the grains to hard slabs. An urgent trilling emitted from its blowhole. Terrified, the girl flung pearls and shells at the beast. Where the fin should have been was an extended tail. This splashed the water to high waves and ploughed the sand into banks and furrows. Rigid with fright, she gazed fearfully up to its gaping, cavernous mouth.

Clement had turned to look back to the dilapidated tenement. In the distance was the south side of the block, with its rows of anonymous, paint-peeling windows. And behind one of those – every detail seen there with a sharp clarity – stood a man with a strange moustache, pinched cheeks and drooping eyelids. Overlaid was a beach and a ruffled sea, with a female running. If only her name could be remembered she would be safe, he knew, but it refused to come to mind.

Even while pondering, Clement viewed the massive creature lumbering away, and as the swooning young woman dangled like a rag doll from its mouth, the whale moved into the churning water and sank beneath the waves.

Clement shrugged and walked along the pavement's gutter, oblivious to his surroundings, locked within himself once more.

Lucid? I'm always lucid. What do you take me for, a sleepwalker? Quite aware of the supposed road I travel along within this blurred day. And I can open another mindroom, if you really insist. Such happy memory filmics in this particular vault. And they can be relived, dwelled within as I like. Far superior to your unreal realness, doctor. You tell me I've a photographic memory like a video camera and tape recorder inside? Correction for you here. I have a multi-dimensional holographic reality within, there ever since childhood.

Here I am, tottering on spindly legs. Heat drunk with the stifling, airless oven the summer patio has become. Standing on tiptoe at grandmother's outhouse window. Lawnmower inside, grass-stained and flaking paint; tins of varnish, cartons of premier elastic bands, cobwebs. There's the mangle mounted on the washing tub. I used to like watching her pull sopping articles from the tub, the clothes somehow reproducing within that primordial broth of scummy water.

I've taken a few grapes and now rolling them through the cylinders of rubber. Surely a clever youngster, changing the mangle to a wine press.

A toy figure in my pocket. When I'm ready I'll feed it into those rollers. This can be symbolic as well. It's not Aaron's physical body, understand, it's his will to exist being crushed.

The dividing wall between the gardens is white and blinding in radiant sunshine. Baskets of petunias hang from it. There, the blooms dusky pink spots. See them? You can't, not yet, I know.

Let me demonstrate my mental power. I'll create the flowers

out of paper. Watch as I refashion this mindroom. Try to understand, doctor. If I looked outside on my grandmother's patio today, the hanging baskets would be overflowing with origami flowers. You realise how wonderful this is? By amending mindrooms I can eventually amend the weaker outer reality.

Here's one of my earliest filmics at that young age when chair legs can be a forest or tables an encampment. Nestling my chin onto folded arms to watch mother perform another miracle of creation.

She is taping a table tennis ball to a cardboard tube, covering them with cotton wool, applying beads down its length. The representation has become more than its constituent parts. Mother is bringing into being a living snowman, tiny but real. For all I knew then, it was being created in a similar way to how she had created me. I'm unable to look away from her active digits as buttons became a nose and innocent organs of sight. The finale produces a yearning for him: a simple piece of string becomes a friendship grin. I hold the snowman close for protection. I whisper to him a secret before he stands above the fireplace, content in the knowledge that the snowman will live forever in the safety and warmth of the house.

Are all tragedies sudden, so horribly abrupt? Can't think of much worse. I'll explain what's happening next: lifting articles from the mantlepiece, mother is polishing the ceramic tiles with a cloth held in the other hand. For a fraction of a second she holds him. But still she's unfeeling to the small being, his expression unchanged yet different. With a casual flick of the wrist, mother throws her child onto the fire.

How to describe feelings which grip me as the form sizzles and becomes one with the flames? I'm mewling as though the world has collapsed, running to the fireplace, and would jump into the fire if it could help. But already the skin of cotton wool is consumed from the cardboard. Button eyes are crying tears of molten plastic. The rubber bands of vitality, for its intestines, sputter and squirm.

This should mortify my senses, shrivel hope. Though we have a reserve of resilience to start afresh. Don't we? Doctor, have I been answering your devious interrogations? I'm able to amend this mindroom but never bother. Perhaps enough to have the name Aaron burn in the fire. I'll lock this room again and put a mud barrier there.

With a gust throwing a handful of rain to the windscreen, Bernadette laughs at the story of the snowman. She's failing to appreciate the delicacy of juvenile emotions involved. I might have left seeds of doubt as to the weight of my mentality. And those seeds could grow into strangling weeds, to obscure understanding and respect. I'll not open those filmics in that particular mindroom anymore, not to anyone.

Bernadette is repeating her question in this happier mindroom, doctor, listen: 'I said, deaf ears, what else did you do when you were young?'

'Oh, the usual. Jelly and ice cream birthdays, tonsillitis every February.' Then a clutter of false memories which should never be recalled. I'll turn on the wipers. 'Why does it always decide to rain at the weekend?'

The road has started a steep decline, winding its way down to the seafront where the line of hotels and souvenir shops are witness to slow-moving waves in a pearl and pale sea. I'll change gear.

A track halfway down the hill has caught my attention. With a twist of the steering wheel the car is crunching gravel. Flattened grass; we've stopped in front of a wide gate.

'What're you doing?' She has twisted in the car seat.

'Intuition and impulse.'

'We were going further along the coast. Won't catch the sea in the middle of boring trees. It's just the dingy woods.' She's inspecting my face without blinking, waiting for an answer.

I lift her chin and peck her on the nose. 'I'll have you know, these woods are owned by King Smythe.'

'What's that about, a weird secret you don't tell anyone?'

'Lord of the woodlands. A king with an enormous crimson head full of understanding.' Sure I never said that.

'It's raining. We can't have a picnic here. I'll get soggy sandwiches and a wet behind. And I can bet King whatever won't come running out with a brolly.'

'Check out the branches.' If only you'd see there, doctor, the track leading from gate to the woods. Trees ahead arch their limbs to make a leafy tunnel. 'A natural umbrella.'

She's leaning forward, squinting through the watery car window. 'The sign: trespassers will be prosecuted.' I'd seen it earlier but kept quiet. 'That's it. Let's go, Donald, the rain might stop by the time we've found another spot.'

Already I'm out of the car and opened the rear door, fighting with the hamper. Bernadette is sulking, I'm certain. 'Cheer up, Binny. Out you get, the water's lovely.'

And it is lovely. Cool raindrops; distant sea calling out its endless story, punctuated by the cries of seagulls. Pattering of the shower on leaves; melodies of birds secreted in the greenness. We are the new Adam and Eve, ideal mates, bound together in our new world. It's as though, with road and car out of vision, nature has overtaken. Could happen.

Cracks would appear on the motorways with thistle and mallow pushing their way through tarmac. Creepers and ivy might begin to shroud bridges and walkways. Wooden fences along the verges will come to life and begin sprouting. On the fields would be saplings of cedar, beech and oak. Floorboards could germinate, eventually pushing fingers of green through carpets; wooden furniture growing branches. Wallpaper peeling away in sodden strips to leave walls to be covered with lichens.

I can visualise this clearly, prepare the three-dimensional mindroom to become outer reality. We'll be protected by a glass bubble made from a special transparent foil. No bad waves or webs will ever penetrate. Happiness always – an everyday ecstacy – and protected inside our wondrous domain. This gift of mine will be the heavenly place for both of us to exist in the dream real, my wonderful Bernadette.

Outside, herds of unattended cattle might roam the streets. The police would exchange truncheons for machetes to clear paths for pedestrians. Macaws and red-plumed parrots will screech and squawk from gigantic trees. There'll be alligators scuttling from sewers, clamping their serrated jaws tightly about the guilty passerby, dragging him screaming beneath the overgrown city. The man with guilt is Aaron. Bernadette will never meet him, his name already burnt away. This is called sculpting reality, Dr Leibkov. I'll teach you one day.

We'll have guardians – bullfrogs, the size of cannonballs. They'll sit with bulging throats and razor-sharp teeth, awaiting any other guilty ones who investigate those green-warted creatures. Other citizens will survive by trapping wild animals hiding in the street-jungles. When houses and concrete tower blocks finally crumble, habitations will need to be built within the relative safety of the tree branches, accommodating a lofty community of pelt-clad savages swinging from vines. Clans will fight for possessions and superiority with bare hands and lumps of timber. They'll lose civilisation little by little until language is lost, communicating with roars, grunts and howls, grimaces and grins. Regressing, growing hair on their bodies; craniums shrinking as frontal lobes do the same, chins becoming weaker, the original man revealed, naked…

'Is there something wrong with you?'

4

Clement stood in a daze in front of the ticket office window at a train station. 'Pardon?' he replied at last.

'Hurry up or clear off.' The clerk was sullen and put his ear closer to the grille.

'I see.' Clement turned to view the faulty ticket machines then to the vertical boarding of the hall blemished by graffiti scrawls. A digital clock changed its numbers to the next hour. His attention was held there until an urgent barking cough distracted him. A queue had formed behind.

It seemed to him that the members of the queue were complicated clockwork machines full of cogs and gears, stuffed with levers and rods, each run down at the same moment. He had the urge to ruffle through their hair like a twitching marmoset would and was sure he would find coin slots underneath, or check their backs for large keys projecting from shoulder blades like cast-iron wings.

'Get a move on,' said the man who had coughed. He let out a shuddering groan of frustration. 'I've got a train to catch, haven't you?'

The others twittered together, exchanging glances and ill-tempered stares, annoyance promoting them to curses and threats.

A businessman left his place in the queue. 'You ought to be put down,' he bawled, accenting his words with a thumb prodding Clement's sternum. 'I've got an extremely important meeting.' He held up a leather briefcase as if in proof. 'Now get out of my way.' His pronouncement seemed to activate the others. They wriggled and nodded in agreement or shuffled on the spot. Clement was certain the ticket hall was sharper with grinding and whirring sounds.

Clement had ignored the businessman's tirade. More concerned with the jabs to his person, a sudden lucidity came over him:

How dare you poke me. I'm not a helpless animal in the animal zoo. I'm human animal unlike you with that stupid toupee, starched collar, arrogant briefcase. Lighten up, construction; accept the truth. Let it cross your electronic grey matter – you build on a sieve. Your months and years become as anonymous as flickering stars, finally snuffed out as easily as a candle. Yet I'm able to manipulate time, slow it down, get it right, repair. Then I'll replay. My required dream becomes real. Are you getting this?

A train announcement had ended and the clockwork queue

had run down, each member standing glassy-eyed and furrow-browed. The clerk in the ticket office was tapping the dividing window glass with a coin: '...otherwise I'll get the stationmaster to sort you out.'

Clement quickly stated his destination and after paying for a ticket he went through the barrier, heading for the platform.

'About time,' someone said.

He wandered between the awaiting passengers. A woman stood up from one of the benches. Clement sat on the vacated seat, squeezing in between a man with large sideburns and a schoolboy who fiddled with the clips on his homework bag. As the boy took out an electronic device, Clement became concerned. He stood and walked further along the platform.

The majority of those waiting were silent, gloved hands, creating breath clouds from their rigid mouths. The start to another week on a cold, unfriendly morning.

Three teenagers broke the quietness. And as they swaggered along the platform clutching mobile phones they threw aside mocking glances. They nudged at each other while passing Clement, staring at his tights moulded to his skinny calves. Their laughter became high-pitched giggles, more at home in young girls' throats than their own. To Clement the hilarity came from two starlings skillfully chasing each other through the chill air. After spiralling and diving, the birds flew over the tracks, then under the walkway bridging the platforms. The laughter went with them. The town's traffic hummed.

A crane's boom, lofty from a building site next to the station, began to scrape through the sky. Hanging at the end were steel cables which, from Clement's distance from them, could have been silk threads; the clank of metal.

That noise, probably made by a dumper truck, altered in volume, the distance making it quieter, sounding like a product of a metallic muzzle. The mind can deceive itself, I have to be careful. Like spitting of bacon fat heard as rain or thunder as a growling leopard in a cave. Squeal of a car's brake pads the call of a wood pigeon. Or was it a partridge? Difficult to tell. I'm not good at analyzing birdsong. I almost believe the woods do belong to King Smythe; it holds a magical quality.

I must call out to Bernadette. 'Catch up.'

'Remember my legs aren't as long as yours.'

King Smythe must have sent an advance party to shine the leaves and spray them a fresh green. He ordered the rain away. No jangling resonances or renegade frequencies within this forest. The sun has to push its way through the canopy of top branches and spots the tracks with silvery puddles of light.

Between bushes and trees, a tangle of ferns and sticks litter the ground. This track is spongy with layers of decaying leaves mulching into the earth.

Bernadette has caught up.

Turning my attention to the hamper. 'Want a go carrying it?'

'Charming, very chivalrous. Look, I wonder who had the nerve?' A smallish crater with flints and tubers poking from its sides. Are you really trying to see, doctor? You seem unresponsive sometimes. Within the crater is a gnarled tree, blackened by fire and smoke. Branches are twisted into grotesque shapes, like knobbly arms reaching out with fingers rigid in palsy, as though the tree had writhed in agony when the flames were upon it. I'll make it writhe again like a blackened exotic dancer.

This track is beginning an incline. Roots exposed on the hill provide us with natural steps. A stream chattering over there. A dappled birch ahead of us marks the summit of the climb.

No longer a definite track. We'll hike on in silence, both of us with reverence to this cathedral of nature. Untidy angles of tree trunks about us. A constant cracking of twigs as we tread, and the whispering leaves. The breeze gentle in this secret, sacred place.

Tang of earth, with a faint odour of cabbages – from fields to the east, I suspect. I've disturbed a gathering of toadstools by accidentally kicking off their caps. I'll pull a fern from the ground to wave away a cloud of midges.

A fallen tree in our path with its foliage dried and shrivelled. I'm going to sit upon the mossed trunk to rest. Bernadette is tramping past.

'Where you going so fast? Hang on, wait.'

I'll have to adjust the strap of the hamper; when it's balanced on my back again, I'll be able to catch up.

Hear her calling back. 'No time for resting. Shift yourself, lazy.'

She is singing. You're trying to listen, I know. The voice crystalline, though not possessing exact pitch or intonation, taking on a melancholic feel.

This woman I make love to – the only one I adore and cherish – is lively and inquisitive, as vital as the rain we have left behind. She keeps appearing, spotted with flecks of light then hidden by tree pillars. The further away into the woods she walks the less she appears. I'm captivated: those hips gyrate as she steps over obstacles or bends to avoid low hanging tree limbs, the hem of her salmon pink dress swinging. The dress is resonating in a quite stunning way in comparison to the greens and browns. Could be neon.

She's phantom, ethereal, eternal. She has become painted over. I must break from this dreaminess, I have to pursue her. This is her game, for me to fight branches which slap or trip. Hack aside brambles and lakes of nettles, step over logs and horse droppings. She might have become a story or an invention though I'm certain that can't happen here. It's simply because she's chosen a better course through the woods.

Watching her go, she was the essence of femininity – graceful and precise – while my progress is slow and clumsy.

'Bernadette, where've you got to?' No use asking you, doctor.

Have to stop. What a noisy banging and crashing I've been making. A hush descending with an ominous quality about it. Movements still play high up in the topmost branches.

'Binny – hello…' No answer. She should answer.

A bank of earth ahead, with shafts of light pushed into this subdued underworld.

Run to it and scramble up. Doctor, are you watching? I'll need to clutch at those stems to aid my ascent. This trouble I'm having – it's not very steep but the hamper is hampering me.

What a splendid surprise. I wish you could see this. All is washed with an exquisite brightness. Abundant bottle-green ferns, growing each side of a wide track covered in a lush moss. Fewer trees but each seem a flawless specimen, huge rugged boles which two adults couldn't encircle. Long dipped boughs are an invitation to be climbed if I were younger. The ferns are neighbours with fields of ox-eye daisies and vibrant red poppies.

As lovely as this is I'm feeling uneasy at losing her. She's here in the mindroom somewhere. Maybe I just need to reconstruct her in a proper fashion; perhaps I need to call her name again.

Push my way through the ferns. Another surprise. A circle of grass surrounding a mammoth oak is in superb condition as if tended by a gardener. A magpie has flown to a bough.

'Bernadette!' Has she got lost?

Throw the hamper onto the grass. I'm certain she's nearby. Make my way back to the shady territory.

As I'm battling through bushes, scraping past black and green thickets, a sense of foreboding is taking hold. This twilight is muffling the outer world. My one spot of woodland is an island, a crafty hall of mirrors reflecting only a few clumps of trees and the same tangles of plants bedded into their layer of decaying vegetation. And if I were to scrape away at my feet I would discover concrete. In fact, when I look down, it is concrete. When I find Bernadette I'll see other Bernadettes running. First there'll be a laugh of delight, hanging high with the birds' nests, solidifying and proclaiming delighted attention, as though suspended on an invisible wire. Then this'll fragment like a comet breaking up; I wouldn't know whether a duplication or the real Bernadette produced it, the wonderful, gentle creature whom I love so much. And she loves me.

Now it's a Bernadette wandering through a dismal place, no doubt with tears welling, desperate to erase false memories of bony fingers shuffling Tarot cards, stealers who can make their skins the texture of bark, chameleon-like. She might be calling from the depths but the scheming trees would be stifling her or sending her in the wrong direction.

Being fooled by these mirrors and I'm going round in circles. I've been hacking aside cables and metal lattices for over ten minutes. Concrete trees and steel bushes decide where I should go; pushing me one way, barring my advance another. Scratched and whipped, rendered tired and impatient, hungry and worried. Must regard my watches. One second needs to kickstart the other.

Try to push away nasty notions. There are some odd

characters about. What if Bernadette has been discovered by someone, this pretty young woman wearing a pretty dress? Perhaps ancient fathers have found her. No, erase that.

As it happens, there's an odd character inspecting me in a quite annoying manner. He appears to be standing on a train station platform. Why would you inspect me in such an aggressive way, Dr Leibkov? I see, it can't be you, the stupid apparition's walked away.

There's the bank I'll climb again. Call out her name once more. I have to. The only reply is that stuttering bird's cry and a flurry of wings.

5

Found the carpet of moss again. Veering off, flattening another channel through the ferns. Walking further until I see the poppies and daisies over to the right and glimmers of sea through the clusters of trees lining the cliff edge.

The pool of pastoral grass; thick roots of the oak tree like embracing knuckles. The hamper open and a picnic laid out: bowl of strawberries and plate of sandwiches, tomatoes, pâté and sticks of celery, on a chequered cloth. And my Bernadette there on the grass, sitting with bare legs curled to the side, holding a glass of wine.

'Binny, where the heck have you been? Was so worried.'

Getting to me, it really has. I was beginning to believe you'd ceased to exist. This mindroom was in danger, was becoming compromised.

'Brush those bits out of your hair. Look peahead, you've ripped your jacket; you'll put blood on it.'

'Blood?'

'You're bleeding, there, the wrist.' Just above our slingshot band of love and perfect understanding. 'What a state you're in. I doubled back, was following. I was going to jump out, give you a surprise,' she's brushing my wig, 'but you ran off again. I've eaten most of the sandwiches, it's your own fault.'

Dabbing smears from my face with a handkerchief.

'No, leave it.' She doesn't understand homage makeup.

'I was only joking.'

'About what?'

'Eating the sandwiches. I've only eaten my half.'

I must throw myself at her as a wave of pure joy cleanses me. I plant kisses on her forehead and cheeks. 'Oh Binny, I lost you.' I must cling to my wife, my friend, my meaning of existence. Have to hold tight, make sure I never let go again.

'Silly.' She's pushing me away to take a sip of wine.

Two cabbage whites flitter and twirl. We will create garlands of buttercups to cup the light.

'I love you; love, love, love you.' Distinct laughter, not certain why.

Yes, I see, how can three simple words hold total meaning? They're only syllables strung together. They can't contain the passions and yearnings, the wanting, more than bodily – the blending of minds, a meeting of spirits. Every ounce of me needs to enfold her for always. A shuddering elation is swelling in my throat.

Gently pull her to me, like this, my hands meeting around her. I have her, she has me forever. The joy of knowing her is incomparable. A light breeze is rippling the poppies, making them dance.

'Do you love me?' I had to ask. Damnation, why did I say it? She's pulled away and appears hurt as she bites her lip. 'Sorry.' I'm no better than a beggar cringing in a shop doorway rattling a tin can. I'm not sorry to you though, doctor, in case you were somehow responsible for promoting that question.

Still not clicking despite you seeming an intelligent man, is it? Let me explain another way then. If I get this precise – really accurate – here in the mindrooms, it'll inevitably happen in the real future dream. Perhaps not exactly but the same ambiences and love colours will occur again. I'm working through such an elegant solution.

Excuse me please while I correct the mistake for the next dream time.

There we are. She appears to have brightened.

We'll eat in silence awhile, let our skin tingle in the warmth within the tranquillity of our abundant surroundings.

'Didn't mean to ask, you know. It was an aberration in the mindroom.'

'Don't start.'

'Trying to say, can never live without you.'

Have I said too much again with no mystery or wonder left? What's your opinion, doctor? You can't speak, can you? I haven't heard you speak for months. But then you don't have to. Bernadette is engaging enough. No matter what she says there's deepness and affection, subtle attraction.

'Eat your sandwiches and be quiet. Stop being serious.'

I should leap to my feet, carve a symbol of union into a guardian tree, let Bernadette watch the happening as if I were a performance artist. Though no need. Already she's watching with fondness given in sultry pulses. My Binny, with your lustrous hair, your delicious kissable neck.

We settle, enclosed by wild angelica, tiers of poppies and daisies, canopy of foliage above. Lay kissing, caressing, embracing. Feeling warmth on the back of my neck, insistent burning weight which has stilled blossoms, held trunks tight. Murmur of leaves; distant sea folding and bending, moving as frothed white curtains to the beach. Affirming life-song, high flying dove, far-away breathy, clacking beat of a train.

She must speak softly, quietly: 'This is our place and our secret.'

'Our place and secret, yes – just the three of us.'

'Three?'

'You, me and King Smythe.' That's all.

Rhythm like tribal drums, beating louder, a solid pulse. Shrieking brakes; grinding and banging as though a train has left its track and is plunging from a plume of unreality through the forest, roaring into the trees, barging them aside as skittles and sending frightened birds flocking. The roll of drums is louder still, becoming frenzied as the Goliath machine charges headlong out of control through the woods, sending high trunks creaking and crashing to the ground, letting new light into hushed habitat for the first time in centuries.

This beat is becoming deafening. The engine pulling its carriages, mashing those poppies to pulp. Thundering past, tearing more trees apart. Bernadette, tumble down the bank to safety. The drums are slowing until the train has come to rest at a platform. I seem to be standing on a platform.

Clicking like castanets as train door buttons are pressed, doors sliding open, shuffling commuters boarding, sorting themselves to single files; a guard with his flag raised and a whistle clamped between his teeth; the doors finally shutting. A shrill peep then an electronic bell sounded. The train moved off.

Clement sat by a window on the train. He watched without much interest as the station began sliding away.

He became anxious all at once with his breathing irregular. He was certain he had forgotten something. Of course, he realised quickly, it wasn't something, it was someone. And the solution was elementary. Create Dr Leibkov in a mindroom aligned with the outside.

But there was no need. The doctor stepped out of a wardrobe and was strolling across the walkway above the train, seen as if without a single worry, not one care in the world.

Not a care in the world. You're well. Bernadette's well. I'm well. Doctor, I might speak to you later though I'm sure there won't be any need.

6

The train moved slowly from the station and under the walkway spanning the rails. It went through a short tunnel before coming out between the high walls of a cutting. The carriages set up a rocking motion. A wall moved by, streaked with ragged runs of dampness. The bricks were locked by boxes of mortar, cracked and crumbling. With the train's lazy speed the wall appeared to be endless. Not only a ponderous repetition moving backwards but row upon row upwards. Clement tried to see the top by flattening his cheek to the window. Perhaps the wall soared upwards forever, and maybe it went on and on across the countryside, slicing through towns and villages, dividing houses and public buildings and parks. Conceivably it was an immense brick barrier with the earth as its epicentre, moving out forever to make separate vastnesses dividing the cosmos. Two sides of an infinite coin, yin and yang, Bernadette and Donald. Mrs Froby would like that concept, Clement thought.

It was as if the oppressive walls possessed magnetic fields

capable of pulling back the carriages – already they were decelerating. At this rate he was going to be late for the first day at work.

The train stopped. No morning light between train and wall, only muddy shadows. And this dimness spread thickly through the carriage as the illuminated strips in the ceiling blinked twice and went out.

If only he was capable of opening the window fully and easing out one of the bricks. Maybe no earth compacted behind but a cheering sky.

The train creaked then jolted into movement and began to pick up speed. Brighter again as the walls quickly came to an end and a cold sunlight plunged into the carriages. The brown roofs of a housing estate stretched away and up the side of a valley.

He inspected his fellow passengers. Over to the right, a woman sat, reading a book. In front of Clement, a besuited man intent upon reading his newspaper which shielded him from the sharp morning sun.

Clement leaned forward and announced with excitement in his voice, 'I know you in the material world.'

The middle-aged man in the striped suit brought the newspaper down and with his brow creased, inspected Clement while adjusting his spectacles.

'Do I know you, young lady?'

'Donadette today.'

'Donadette?' He appeared confused and flinched from his

chunk of raw sunshine before taking the spectacles off to clean the lenses with a part of his shirt. Once the glasses were replaced he gave a snort and growled, 'What – the – hell is your game, hmm?' His eyes were enlivened, unsure as to where he should rest his sight.

The auburn wig which Clement wore was cut to a bob. His sallow face, twitching and beige with foundation, had mascara, lipstick and rouge roughly applied. Over his embroidered blouse he wore an overcoat and where this finished was the bottom of a bottle green skirt. From this protruded lumpy knees held together, his skinny legs covered with tights. What appeared as a random pattern were the flattened hairs under them. A pair of women's block heeled sandals were on his feet.

'Remember me, Jeremy? I've got reliable corridors and mindrooms now.' Clement showed a pale palm with a thick green elastic band around his wrist dividing the two watches there.

Keeping his mouth hard as if attempting ventriloquism, Mr Finch replied, 'How do you know my name?' His cheeks had become a flustered red and he looked quickly about the carriage with obvious embarrassment.

'Still at Penshart I'm guessing. Haven't appeared in a while. Where are you living for real this time?'

'I know who you are now. Donald Clement. The one with the — problems. So they've let you out, have they?'

Clement ignored the sarcastic question in favour of extending his hand, the nails there painted with a green varnish. 'That's me. Pleased to see you still exist. And I have solutions.'

'Yes, I'm sure,' was all Finch could reply, avoiding the handshake.

'I lodge in living quarters, an overall womb in Cressmore Street. Do you know, I've forgotten your surname.' Finch, still disturbed by Clement's appearance, was unable to speak. Clement continued, 'Hang on, don't tell me ... Finch, yes? Finch on the fiddle.'

'I beg your pardon?'

'No offence meant, Jeremy,' Clement returned, 'if you didn't realize your label. You know what the workers at Penshart Press were like. Used to call me Don the deranged. Just because they found my theories hard to comprehend. Because I perceive differently. Couldn't understand me wanting to be a scriptwriter. Or discern any transformation. Like today, they wouldn't get it: subduing the inferior haters, destroyers, the perverted minds. I've invited part of the woman for a while, you know, permanent love and understanding, welcoming forgivers and peacemakers. I can actually be anything I want really, since protecting myself. Still doing accounts? Juggling numbers, becoming fat or slim, depending how much you feed them. Sure you get my artistic meaning.'

After a pause, Finch answered with a suspicious tone, 'Actually, I'm executive accountant at Stansbird and Swale. You've heard of them no doubt. Anyway, nice to have met you again but I need to read my paper before the next station.'

Both were having to raise their voices above the clattering of wheels as the carriages changed tracks.

Clement had leant back and was seemingly communicating with his lap. 'Not them with their theatrical fabrication. Willbeam or something. Wilson, was it? I did tell you to forget that travesty, doctor.'

Finch hid behind his newspaper, hands shaking.

'Oh,' said Clement, raising his wigged head. 'Walstaff, that was it. Unreal interruption, supposedly expensive. There, we've come round to those elusive numbers again, haven't we?' Finch buried his back to the seat and let a shrug be answer enough. 'Haven't we?' stated Clement again. A simple enough question.

'Yes,' Finch muttered finally and hurriedly, glancing at his watch then out of the window, willing the train to go faster. 'Well then,' he added, throwing his newspaper beside him, 'Still no better, I see. Where do you work now? Proofreading for the asylum pamphlets perhaps?'

'I remember the printing business. Those greedy machines, floods of colour, enough to paint the town in new shades. Imagine no grey concrete. How pleasant to see it in another vibrancy. Orange, maybe. Don't know what you think.' He nodded, and grinned at his own humour.

'I don't know what *you* think,' Finch said quietly.

'Another for you: eidetic or diuretic?'

'Look, you are feeling alright – you're looked after.'

Clement nodded with a benign appearance taking over.

Finch began to fold his newspaper in preparation to leave at the next stop. The train was already slowing. He regarded Clement and was disconcerted to see him still nodding and grinning.

Clement's former colleague cleared his throat. 'Thanks for an interesting conversation,' he lied. 'Alright then…'

The carriage rocked from side to side as the train slowed the more.

Finch was feeling uncomfortable at the odd expression on Donald Clement's lipstick-painted lips. In an attempt to break the spell of his companion's obsessive behaviour he blurted, 'Sorry about your divorce. I'm sure it worked out to a satisfactory conclusion.'

Clement finally became still. 'Barriers,' he said with a sour look upon him, his coloured eyelids flickering.

Jeremy Finch got to his feet, moving to and fro with the motion of the train. He was gripping a luggage rack. 'Pardon?' he said.

'Dr Leibkov. He's demands I tear them down. Of course, I tell him what sort they've become.' Clement spoke quietly as if imparting secret information: 'Stronger than any metal, they've an opacity quite unlike any solid object. These barriers are such that, by comparison, a boulder or a stove, or the stump of a tree – you name it – is positively transparent.' A line of people hurtling past the window appeared as if they were on some wildly moving platform propelling them past a stationary train. Finch pretended interest of this phenomenon and peered intently out. Clement continued, 'Sometimes I'll let through a small offering, though not often. For instance, it's two-fold and the appointed observer, you see. Since spirals from primordial slime there've been mirrored relationships. Things have dualism or will have, agreed? Perfectly matched pairs, one with its opposite. Synthesis of real with the unreal now. Tell me, is that so bad? What weight of argument have you to accent your reasoning on this matter?'

Clement believed his speaking to be fine and filled with meaning, and was surprised at his own eloquence this early in the morning. He wanted to express his innermost feelings and the compulsion was helped by Finch's listening ears. If only Jeremy would stay longer, he wished, then there would be a discussion of the highest calibre.

The train was slowing to a standstill. Finch was ready to move to the carriage doors. He was trying his best to ignore this colleague of old, the young man who had changed for the worse, who gaped up at him in a disturbingly childlike manner, tapping Finch on the knee with a finger. Dressed as a woman, face caked with make-up. Accentuated movements of the hand, the wrist there with two watches and elastic band, speaking with spirited features without any apparent meaning.

'Forget nonsense, he insists in a definite fashion. But you see I require protection from those spawned ideas because they were like pokers straight out of a fire, or like … like some brutish acid-exuding creature eating me away inside.'

Before the train had finally stopped, Finch stood hurriedly

and went over to punch the door button, willing the doors away. When the train finally came to a standstill and the doors slid open he leapt out of the carriage, nearly losing his balance as he pushed his way through the lines of awaiting passengers. 'Out of my way,' he ordered.

Clement had stood to walk to the automatic doors and was leaning out. 'It's alright, Jeremy,' he shouted after him over the heads, 'barriers can't hurt. Quite the opposite. They're for inspired protection. Nice to meet you again, goodbye.'

'Move please,' stated an elderly man from the platform.

Clement nodded with a friendly expression and moved further inside the carriage to allow the traveller to alight. The man stepped up in a cumbersome way and stood panting.

1

You are a real one. I can discover immediately what sort of person you are from just a few seconds of analysis. See into you as easily as looking through clear glass. For example, your ancestors would have lolled under eucalyptus trees, instilling in their genes a lethargy which would impart certain physical attributes to future generations.

You're an ageing version with a sunken chest. Jacket shining with patches of grease. What hair you have is sickly like the leaves of a wilting plant. And those rusted fingers – a heavy smoker, no doubt.

You bloat yourself with beer and scotch, take up that reality space there in the corner leading to the beer garden. Sucking on a miserable bit of rolled paper, meagre strands of tobacco lining the inside. And a vile slurping when you drink. Rattling cough as though your lungs are about to liquidize, to come out onto the stained handkerchief clutched to your mouth.

'Can't you say anything? I think he's positively disgusting.'

I agree with Bernadette; weaving my way between the

empty tables to the bar counter.

There's Daniel behind the bar, checking stocks, pointing a pencil to a barrel of sherry. 'Already? You're good for business today.'

'No thanks, not yet.' I'll sit on a stool and rest elbows on the counter soakmat. I see you, doctor, and Daniel's double with slicked hair, and part of my face, given back from a piece of mirror not covered with glinting bottles and optics. You can be the ambient one reflected. 'The scruffy guy in the corner. Well, to be honest he's a bit dirty, isn't he?'

'The old boy's here every afternoon; waits outside for the doors to be unlocked. He'll have his ale and be gone. Quite harmless. Been coming here for years. One of the locals.'

I have an admiration for the doddering duffer. Fifty minutes of brown ale is his meaning of existence. He has this daily ritual, an ambition if you like, as modest as it is. An excellent obsession perhaps. His life is there in the glass and cigarettes and corner.

Daniel is tapping his top teeth with the pencil. I know you can't see much from where you are, Dr Leibkov, on the walkway, in the mirror, in a bar of the Neptune Hotel.

'Who is he, then?'

The barman nodding towards the opposite corner to where the old man sits. You stay behind, inverted laterally, doctor. You can listen from there. I'll be over by the red oak panelling, looking back to judge Daniel's aim.

'What, this?' Placing a finger onto a brass ship's clock,

shining but deceased. A shake of the head.

I'll take a step away from the boat wheel to survey the whole wall. On one of the shelves, a stuffed halibut in the safety of its case. Below, in another glass case, is presented the long twisted horn from a narwhal. A grubby stuffed fox – which might once have been a taxidermist's masterpiece – glares as it sinks on its patchy haunches by the coat stand. The rest of the wall is covered with yellowing engravings, paintings and sepia photographs, and a fine layer of dust.

I shall be your perception again, my psychiatric shaman. I'll put my nose close to one of the engravings. There's the studious workmanship of lines. Step back a little and the picture becomes alive with tonal variations though produced only with black ink on white parchment.

Thrashing spikes of the sea pushing and dragging at a lifeboat. The helmsman clutching a rope to the rudder, a petrified girl huddling in the comfort of another. Roaring waves, shrieks of wind, sobs of a women quivering amidst twelve others. An oilskinned sailor struggling with the oars, trying to gain purchase with the blades in the violent waters, the side of the doomed ship looming beside them. A mother still on the ship's deck, her child wrenched from her. Others fight like wounded animals, scratching and biting, tearing at each other's clothing, the struggle for survival, primitive impulses driving them. Creaking of the sails, splintering snap as the bowsprit is broken, a despondent song from the rigging, impotent cries of those left behind to die. One struggling vainly with the ship's wheel, another holding his comrade upright, yet another clinging to the boom which had lowered the lifeboat, reaching out imploringly, his life about to be taken by those mountains of water, the mindlessly animated vastness of ocean...

'No, not that one. Next to it.'

A small photo, showing portside of a fishing smack snuggled to the side of a jetty, the sea behind placid and sunlit. A younger version of the spitting man in the corner sits mending nets. He's surrounded by lobster pots and yards of mesh. Smoke from the briar clamped between his teeth.

I must call over to Bernadette. 'Come and have a look.' She's pretending not to hear as she reaches for her drink.

The fisherman made an uneasy truce with the sea to reap a harvest of fish and lobsters. He deserves his prominence and distinction: a crown of amethyst shells, sea flowers and coral armour. He will become semi-transparent – like a jellyfish – to blend with his mighty ocean and all it contains.

Under that beam spanning the bar, holding lanterns and a bell, the impressive figurehead stands painted in its bold colours. The heavy chunks of timber glued and carved into a winged messenger, its shoulders hunched forward: it's the fisherman's sea-soaked shoulders. Across the brown ceiling, covered with shrivelled starfish and compasses, there are paddles and clumps of rope; glance back over to the engraving – there he is again as the captain of the doomed vessel, superior resignation upon him, standing as still as a boulder while others are madness about.

And there you were in the corner by the ornate fireplace hung with brass, gone to your Atlantis to be with your willing sirens and mermaids, until tomorrow morning when you'll return for your pint of brown ale.

'You here again? Twice in one day?'

A group of tourists are arranged in the wise fisherman's province. They sway drunkenly from side to side singing a bawdy ballad, the throb of a train's wheels acting as metronome.

'My wife went off to do shopping and a wander round the antiques.' An explosion of laughter from another quarter. 'Can't be bothered with that stuff.'

'Three, four, five pounds; thanks.' The hand receiving the change retracts into the forest of customers lining the bar.

'What's the time? Quarter to seven; I'll down another swift one before I pick her up. Give it another three quarters of an hour. It'll do my headache good anyhow. I don't think the market shuts until half eight; and I'll be on this train for a while longer. Mine's the usual when you're ready.'

Raucous laughter, someone sobbing with tears of mirth and slapping their thigh. Every table top invisible under a layer of glass jugs, plates, snack packets. You've put your pint away pretty smartish for a doctor. Another quick one then. A hyena cackle, bubbling murmurs, whooping buoyant airs. These shaking heads, those nodding ones. Hyena for a second time then a trumpeting elephant. Baboons still rock in the corner; a whinnying horse or should it be a seahorse? If I drink quickly there should be no worries. With clicking dominoes and thudding darts into the board, this is becoming a bit hazy. Congealing into one growling babble. Riff-raff are jostling me. Try as I might I can't gain any enjoyment from watching the darts players though I'll take one of their sandwiches on offer. Tastes of puffed mush. Look, someone's drunk my beer by accident, already it's finished. One more hop-bittersweet frothing pint, just to round off the evening, shouldn't matter. The anchor bolted to the oak panelling is sliding down, I'm convinced. If I was to use my imagination more, I'd persuade myself we're not in a bar of the Neptune Hotel in a train carriage but inside of a whale. If only I could focus enough to see the time from the clock above the fruit machine. It's registered, beer equals doctor, both dissolve barriers. These stupid false memories barging in, beginning to create inebriated tears. Quickly dismiss them. Let them percolate through this zoo, the babbling mixture with flashing teeth and chinking glasses, while everyone is treading into puddles. Maybe it's their drinks slopped to the floorboards. But it can't be, the pools have quickly joined and the drinkers stand or sit in two inches of water. Not that anyone seems concerned, they continue their raucous banter. Glimmering water has risen more; it's level with their knees and fast rising still. This liquid of the fourth pint has rendered my face numb. Water laps at the table edges. Splashes when hit with a drop of the arm or sharp movement of the hand. A bottle of beer bobbing past. There's the barman, quite unconcerned, taking money from a customer and casually wiping slops from the counter. Now holding tongs clutching ice cubes but strangely at the other end of the bar now, pulling on a pump again. And the gabbling and gossiping goes on, the waffling and singing, heavy drone of a million flies in this deceptive room; clapping hands, insidious ale still poured down their forgiving throats, the subterraneans unaware of the communal bath rippling about their necks. And this chilly water has taken feeling from my arm. I must try to move it though progress is sluggish as the whole of me has been reduced to slow motion. But there at last, as dregs of ale run from the bottom of the glass, the waters have reached the dusty ceiling and completely covers all. And there's time enough to watch a ponderously moving crowd with sounds muffled and echoing, bubble streams rising from their noses. Mark them move like sea plants wafted by currents before the vile taste of salt-bitter liquid rushes down my gullet, making me want to vomit. 'Excuse me,' I must insist as I swim through these smirking crowds, plastering a hand across my mouth as stomach heaves, turning over like a cement mixer, threatening to eject its contents. 'Excuse me,' as I sway up to the pub entrance which is rippling in that unnatural way underwater…

'Excuse me.'

8

Clement's eyes sprang open. A young mother was leaning toward him.

'Would you be so kind?' she asked, flicking her sight in the direction of the train window. Heating from below the carriage seats was becoming stifling.

'Yes, of course.'

He stood and put fingers on the metal catch at the top of the smaller pane to open it.

'Say thank you to the nice person, Emily,' the woman said before clasping one of her children's hands in her own.

The young girl's large eyes, as blue as cornflowers, dominated her petite round face. With delicate fingers she had hold of her fish-shaped toy. She wriggled her nose and looked to dimpled knees then to the countryside speeding past.

Her younger brother clutched a stick. On the end of the stick was a brightly-coloured bird made of plastic. The boy put the tail of it to his lips and blew it as a whistle, a pleasant chirruping produced amidst the dull rapping of the wheels along a dull landscape with its dull bushes, then a valley of dull pint pot houses and winter-ravaged trees.

Clement blinked slowly. If only we could wish to remain as we were in our early years, he thought. Instead, minds and bodies are contaminated, innocence stolen; victims of fate and time.

It was not the physical aspects of ageing he detested, more the forgetting of wholesome laughter, the purity and optimism. The ability to repel harmful rays without the need for tin foil. Children should be admired for these things – he reasoned – and we should be allowed a little envy.

Wondrous stories of what should be, the real dream, free from hatred and malice; learn to be pure with love. As is the powerful love for my Bernadette, he explained to the remembered psychiatrist.

Still the world appeared to Clement as if seen through dark glasses, rendered gloomy and dismal. Sooty-barked trees with limp leaves, grey parks strewn with rubbish and lakes like sores, pylons striding across a sombre landscape. Then a factory complex with its zig-zag roofed warehouses, walls of dun-toned corrugation surrounded by joists and piles of gravel. And forklift trucks moving here and there between canisters, looking like yellow beetles, nest-building. More sterile stretches of concrete, barren streets, anonymous houses with stark slips of unkempt garden.

Clattering of wheels on the track; tiredness, the oppressive heating…

The window tapped, perhaps with a metal object.

This mindroom is hazy. Not certain it should be active. It's only with a forced effort that I'm able to see. Eyelids are somehow connected to a titanium mask fitted over face and scalp. And as my swollen eyes open they activate a vacuum. This tightens the mask giving me an acute pain. It seems to be making my brain ache – a pounding as though a heart pumping blood. Now I'm seeing properly: it's Bernadette. Have to fumble for the key to open the car window. But she's screaming at me.

'Don't open the window, open the damned door you drunken fool.'

Please Bernadette, change that line.

She is pushing me towards the passenger seat. I'll have to climb over the gear stick. She's out of the car again and opening a rear door, flung two shopping bags into the back. Lights from The Neptune Hotel are throwing a yellow stain over the forecourt. The sea is listening from the seafront behind the hotel.

Bernadette's bottom lip quivers as she holds out her palm for the ignition key. Searching in my pockets, still drunk and having great difficulty in coordinating my actions. A halfwit here, I know. I'll make it better next time.

You can be a wise night owl, doctor. Follow us.

The car is coughing, moving up the incline away from the town. Engine is roaring against the pull of gravity on this steep country road. Bernadette changes down to second gear. She's gripping the steering wheel tightly and staring ahead without a single blink. We're at the zenith of the hill. The road has levelled out. This night is crowding us and becoming a weighted load. The headlights are cutting a white channel ahead. A segment of pastey moon casting weak illumination. Bernadette still silent. I'm trying to speak but my tongue is made of papier-mâché; lips have desiccated. Must close burning eyes but the seat is revolving fast. I'm strapped helplessly in it, like on a funfair ride. Feeling ill with drink and despair, and self-recrimination.

This mindroom needs much repair.

I turn to look at a pulsating Bernadette. This action makes a steel ball roll inside my cranium, already leaden, already too heavy for my neck to support. Bangs at my temples. A light is emanating from her, impregnable.

'Let me explain,' I've managed to say, sounding strangled and pathetic.

Still she stares impassively ahead, unreachable and resistant. Her hands have organically meshed with the steering wheel.

Buddhists chant for days to achieve a heightened state of being. But all I have to do is bend over the lavatory pan, hands on knees, and throw up. Feel the jerking contractions of diaphragm and burning in my gullet. Gasp in between spewing. Pull the flush. The vortex of water might as well be my mental state. I'll have to swill.

Switch the controllers off.

'Thank you very much. I was watching that film.' She's scowling. Never seen that expression from her before. The blank television screen crackles with static. Needs covering with tin foil. I'll amend that.

'Talking to me, are you?' I had to say it.

'You were dribbling my name and sulking. What was the point?'

'Give me a break, I drank a bit too much. Really am sorry, alright? Finally been sick so I feel clearer.'

'Suppose I'm meant to forgive you.' No, Bernadette, you say something different. 'You knew you had to pick me up at half past seven. I think you must be brain-dead sometimes.'

Just seen for the first time this evening the pads of puffed skin beneath her eyes. She must have been crying.

This significant event must be stopped. I'll think on other subjects. Lock this catastrophe of a mindroom and place a heavy barrier until I can repair properly.

Whales once had hind legs. How remarkable that would have been. They have rudimentary bones in those massive carcasses, corresponding to hind limbs and a pelvic girdle.

Stop…

'How could you, Donald. I was getting scared, waiting outside of the mall at night. And all you did was get out of your head.' She's on her feet.

'Not fair.' I've made Bernadette draw in breath. 'Let me explain, there's daylight until nine.'

'Oh I see. Alright to leave me waiting because the moon hadn't come out.'

'I didn't mean that.'

Stop, stop.

'Anyway, thanks. I only had to carry the shopping two miles while you were snoring.'

'Two miles? Not that far. Still, I don't understand why you didn't catch a bus or a taxi home.'

'Didn't have any money left. And I couldn't phone, could I, you with your stupid decision to throw the mobile away.' I know the reason, Bernadette. It's the infrared, it can damage. 'Anyhow, what do you mean catch a bus? You were going to pick me up, remember?'

Lock this room, stop us from arguing, stop the sentences from ever being formed; they ring in my ears before I speak but I'm powerless to keep them from evacuating.

'Won't happen again, alright? Just belt up. Anyway, are you so damned perfect?'

These sharp words have pricked her truculent bubble. She's dissolved into tears. She's walking back and forth, wringing her hands. Stop her from doing that, doctor, I can't seem to.

It's done, finished, over. Delete the argument.

This filmic, it should be as easily manipulated as celluloid to edit, ideally to have it erased. This version isn't valid. Can't you see? Could be the beginning of the end if I can't alter it.

Bernadette has plunged her face into a settee cushion to drown her sobbing. And I'm still ranting in front of her, one sentence demanding another to counteract it, frightened to stop gabbling because this would leave a chasm of silence between us.

It's not as though I'm unaware of any impending disaster. I'm only too aware of destroying her image of me. I know I'm rubbing away with a rough sandpaper on our shining relationship. I can sense it's the first domino to topple onto the line of others. Yet I'm still raging – stop, where are my barriers? How can these bleak memories have the power to hide them?

9

'**S**top, whoa.' Bernadette attempting to pull the wine glass away. How did you manage to open one of my mindrooms, doctor? I'm impressed.

'Are you trying to get my daughter tipsy?' That's Bernadette's father talking.

Here's her mother, Elizabeth, about to add a comment from the living room. 'Harold, she doesn't have a birthday every day.'

Bernadette, leaning back on her metal chair by our patio table, pressing the bridge of her sunglasses. Now smiling gently while sipping her white wine. The high afternoon sun is sparkling within the glass. I will make it incandesce the more, like a fireworks sparkler. I'll take sugar cubes from their bowl on the table to make the shape of steps. Now it's a sugar whale. Aromatic smoke dispersing from Harold's pipe. A lawnmower snores from somewhere.

Elizabeth has stepped out onto the sun-washed patio carrying a cake. It's holding twenty-two flame-twitching candles. 'Happy birthday, dear daughter.'

Bernadette is delighted. We'll pull the wine glasses from the table for the cake to sit there.

Elizabeth tuts. 'I've forgotten a knife.'

Bernadette's sister: 'I'll get it.'

A starling is stepping jauntily across the lawn despite the oppressive heat, that purposeful pressure draining the day.

Elizabeth begins humming the traditional birthday ditty. We join in, the last line supplemented by Marianne as she returns from the kitchen with the cake knife.

Another waft of pipe smoke. A baby from over the neighbour's fence is making the pram squeak while paddling its legs. The infant is gurgling and spluttering, vocalizing to the sun.

Elizabeth has cut wedges of the cake.

'No, really,' I have to say.

'Don't be a fuss-pot,' Bernadette tells me.

The pipe-call of a cuckoo. A bumble-bee drones over to the geraniums.

'Delicious,' Marianne has remarked. 'You'll have to give me the recipe.'

'Yes, I will, dear. Harold, eat your cake.'

He grunts a reply while still sucking on his pipe. He has turned to me. 'What are your plans for the garden, Donald?' He's aiming the pipe stem to it.

'Well, the grass has settled in nicely; the circular lawn was Bernadette's idea. Fruit bushes along there. I want to start a vegetable patch down by those shrubs.' I'm waving an arm in that direction. 'You know, lettuce, onions, that sort.'

Marianne is talking excitedly with her sister. They are both giggling. She's admiring one of Bernadette's presents. The pearl earrings sleep in their bed of cotton wool.

A bluebottle has flown lazily onto the back of a chair. I see, doctor, you've made it a wasp. You're getting the hang of this.

'You've missed this one,' Marianne says, pointing to a wrapped box on the patio table.

Bernadette is removing her sunglasses and like an impatient junior snatches at the present. She picks at the tape, cooing eagerly; her long hair has fallen about her beautifully-proportioned face as she tears away the paper and flips open the box.

'Thank you, Donald.'

Standing behind my chair, bending to kiss me on the cheek. She has taken the oval locket from the box and handed it to her sister.

'Really nice, Binny. Isn't it, mum?'

Marianne is holding up the locket by the gold chain and it revolves and catches the light. Spinning fast, seeming to show both sides at the same time. And there − faster still, beginning to blend.

Can't be; how has this conjuring trick come about? The locket has vanished and in its place is an enamelled pendant, round and green, tarnished and encrusted, as though it were a centuries-old coin from the bottom of an ocean. This is making me shake with rage. Get rid of this disgusting materialisation!

Marianne is attaching the chain about Bernadette's neck and there's the gold locket hanging only. I can't regard it in case the vile transformation takes place again.

'Clumsy.'

Wasn't watching where I was putting my big feet. I really must stop putting glasses of wine on the floor. Marianne is running to the kitchen to fetch a sponge.

'Sis, don't worry. It's an old carpet anyway.' Marianne has already returned and is on her knees, sponging at the liquid seeping into the pile.

Harold says, 'We'll think about buying you a new carpet.'

'No,' Bernadette and I have replied in unison. 'Really,' she continues. 'Donald is getting a raise soon.'

'Going well if you're getting a pay rise.'

I'll sit next to him on the settee. The three women are chatting. 'To be honest, the work isn't satisfying enough. Day in, day out, reading copy from somebody else's pen; I wish I'd become a scriptwriter. Still, these mindroom scripts are becoming easier to influence.'

Harold is nodding though I don't think he understands. 'Listen, a good job is scarce nowadays. You must be grateful at having one at all.'

Bernadette interrupts. 'Let's go somewhere.'

'I'm tired, dear.' Elizabeth has fluttered her eyelids as if to underline her comment. 'You go on. I'll catch forty winks.'

Bernadette is holding her hands. 'Come with us, mum — we'll show you the pier again, you'll like it.'

'No, really. Go without me.'

10

I've handed Marianne her candy floss. Pinkness glows from it, creating a sticky tint to smear the clouds and adhere onto beach pebbles and sand, spreading pink over the promenade.

Can't keep my sight from straying to the locket hanging from its chain about Bernadette's neck. It's taunting me. As I regard it, quickly it changes to green. I must rip the chain from her and throw the locket as hard as I'm able.

Flashing in the pink sky from gold to green then to gold again until it plops into the pinky sea.

'Going to put a picture in there?' Marianne asks.

Distant cries of seagulls as they circle the roofs of The Neptune Hotel. See the row of white and cream-fronted hotels, arcades of souvenir shops and amusements, the cluster of antiques stalls. Laughter of children making sandcastles on the beach or the occasional shriek from one of the holidaymakers playing ball in the waves. The stretches of sand are broken by rocky clumps, like scabs. Sunbathers expose their chalky flesh to the mighty sun. Up near the west end of the promenade, a golf course lines the top of the cliffs. Tiny flags are waving from the greens. And there, on an outcrop running far into the gleaming sea is a little finger of a lighthouse.

A maze of backstreets run up and away from the seafront. The whitewashed walls and red tiles are vivid in the afternoon rays. Above the hotels and shops stands Milsley Castle, houses scattered below the crumbling buttresses as though its subjects. Gentle waves are breaking over the beaches.

'Catch up, Donald.' They've walked through an arch – a filigree mass of ironwork – onto the pier. A sound like hissing pistons.

'Do you love me?'

'Donald, stop it, please. I married you, didn't I?' I have got hold of her hand while we wait for her sister and father to come out of the souvenir shop.

But this isn't right. She's there at the end of the pier, entering the small white chalet…

Here again holding my hand while we stand by a lifebelt attached to the iron railings. Her soft hand, perfect and smooth. Made to fit exactly into mine.

'What did you get? Let me see.'

'Binny, it's on my head,' laughs her sister. A sea-breeze plays with the ribbons on Marianne's sunhat. 'What do you think, Donald?' She's striking a model's pose.

'Very snazzy.'

I am leaning on the railings; I've looked away and down. There's a disturbance from under the sea's surface. Bubbles are coming up and joining with scummy broth, and the seaweed wrapped around the legs of the pier. A whirlpool has started, spinning faster as I look, forming a liquid hollow in its centre. The hollow is growing at a surprising rate. Seagulls are flying in circles as though to imitate this whirl of water. Sunbathers have picked up their towels, running to the promenade while seabathers are blown to the beach, each one riding a wave like a surfer. Brilliant cracks striate the dominating arc of sky; gathering smoke-grey clouds are illuminated for seconds before smothering the sun. A ghostly whistling, coming from the gaps in the gangplanks, join forces with the wind moaning like a lament. Flags and pennants along the length of the pier are flapping furiously and their ropes hum. Then without premonition or expectation the waves about the whirlpool are erupting as if there's a volcano underneath. Those sheets of water are being flung into this day-turned-to-night. And it's raining down upon us, drenching me in seconds, nearly washing me off my feet into the turbulent pink waves. There's a roar and so loud it's drowned other sounds. It has raced over to the cliffs in the east and the cliffs has sent a duplicate back. Pedestrians have flung themselves into the arcades, cowering in confused fright. From out of the swirling waters is being thrust the three prongs of a trident, each prong the height of a man. The shaft is following, a seemingly never-ending dynamic barrel of metal. And gripping it is a massive hand. The same hue as coral, larger than a bull elephant. I'll have to hold tightly onto the railings. My fingers are frozen there; sobs are choking my throat; everyone else has been swept overboard. The rest of this titanic phenomenon is bursting forth with such power as to send high waves crashing over the promenade and flooding the roads. Cars are being swept into shop windows. Swells are being sent far off to the horizon. And here before me, like a dream, is Neptune, rising one hundred feet or more. His skin is alive with fish and crabs. His beard and hair are made of seaweed; his crown is coral with jewels from the ocean's vaults. Those whale-like lips are as purple as amethyst, the gigantic eyes as pale blue and opalescent like topaz. You have to see somehow, Dr Leibkov: Neptune pushing his way through the raging currents as easily as if it were the shallow end of a swimming pool. He's reached the end of the pier, no more than a bench to him. He has plucked the white chalet from it and holding it on his outstretched, limpet-encrusted palm. I imagine a miniature man kicking open the door of the pathetic structure, Aaron running out, not onto hard planks but the spongy, olive flesh of that giant hand. With an easy motion the fingers of Neptune have tightened about the chalet. It's disintegrating into matchsticks and pittering the choppy surface of pinkish sea.

'Looking good.' The girls are running excitedly along the gangplanks to the funfair. 'See you later.' That was Bernadette shouting back.

'Fancy a cup of tea?'

Harold's puffing on his pipe and nodding.

I doubt you need a drink, doctor. Anyhow, I'm not sure you deserve one. I'm repairing my past future but you're not helping enough yet.

An announcement telling passengers to change trains broke Clement's dream-like state. Clement stepped off the train and joined the crowded platform. He looked up to the sawtooth slats along the platform canopy then to the ornate brackets holding it but still not really seeing.

Or feeling: he had become a sensationless rind with his insides stone, cold and heavy. And mind adequately clouded. Cloaked in mystery, he estimated. He liked the idea of that. Then wrapped in enigma and covered with barriers. Yet why should they be failing, he asked himself. Had Dr Leibkov's insidious claptrap begun to have an effect and if so, how long before he was damaged?

A shrill whistling: a guard with a whistle still to his lips and a flag held to the wintry air. Clement was bewildered; he turned one hundred and eighty degrees. The other passengers had boarded the train that stood on the opposite side of the platform, save one. She ran past the guard. 'Quickly,' he urged.

The girl was wearing brown leather shoes and black diamond-patterned tights (or stockings, Clement considered in an instant) with an elaborately embroidered cape about her and a salmon pink dress. Her hair was held up with a tortoiseshell hair clip. Fine wisps and a white neck below her bunned hair as she stepped up. Her profile was to him. Unplucked eyebrow, the high cheekbone and pouting mouth: he saw these in a handful of seconds. Clement ran to the same train carriage she had entered, brushing past the guard as he went, his sight never leaving the young woman.

It was Bernadette.

11

Five other people occupied the carriage compartment though Clement's attention was for Bernadette only.

So she did exist again outside him. He wanted to hug her close, smell her scent.

By impulse, he looked to her feet. The shoes there were not brown leather. The legs and the tights were as he had seen them though the calves seemed plumper than remembered. The salmon pink dress was neither pink nor a dress, but a mustard-coloured pleated skirt. She was undoing her cape which, Clement noticed, was secured by buttons.

This person was not Bernadette after all. A similarity in facial structure maybe but inspecting her annoyed face with its different nose, smaller eyes and thinner top lip, this woman was a mere caricature. Clement resolved to smother his sight, suddenly swamped with fatigue.

He inexplicably found an erotic scene flashed into his inner view: a woman seductively draped in silken ribbons, laying on her back upon a Persian carpet. This sculptured carpet was made with the finest of dyed silks, the pile cut to different heights, intriguing symbols in pastel shades within it. The woman's head lay as smooth and featureless as an egg, propped up with large pillows. These pillows glinted and caught light; they refracted luminosity, splitting it into prism colours which altered the shades of the carpet in streaks and spots as though a reacting chemical had been spilt there. She was surrounded by lakes of poppies and bright daisies. Some of the mustard and red flowers, being flattened by the carpet, lay poking out from around its perimeter, their petals limp and stems snapped, or bent and oozing a resinous sap. About her, a summer brightness. Beyond this incandescent bubble was a night sky peppered with stars. Her breathing was deep. She felt her shoulders before moving both hands down, caressingly, to the cleft between her ample breasts which rose and fell with each breathe. Rhythmic sighs left her as gentle as the susurration of autumn leaves, the scintillating pillows beneath her letting out clouds of white points like sparks flying from a bonfire. The exotic carpet undulated and rippled, the brightness waxed and waned. Her sighs became the wind and it blew in bursts, making the luminous fields of flowers bow and quiver. And there, leaving a furrow behind him, a black-moustached figure walking closer. He wore a striped jacket. The faceless woman breathed faster as though she sensed the nearness of him.

Arrest the man's advance: manipulate sparks from the pillows to form walls, instruct these to surround the woman, to hide and protect her from the advancing man. Let pale green stars grow until they overlap, becoming a ceiling above.

This mindroom I know; it has been developed and tailored to perfection. Bernadette is laying on the bed next to me. With her elbow buried in the pillow and her upturned palm forming a plinth for the side of her head, she's flicking through a magazine. The evening sun seems loathe to rest, still feeling as hot as the afternoon.

'My skin's glowing, look. Do you think I've tanned?'

The walls shimmer; the eiderdown has become perfumed satin sheets as large as the largest of rooms, as smooth as cream. This space can be an art gallery with dimmed spotlights, white wine trickling down granite walls and over gilded picture frames. Entrances at either end are sealed with large cubes of red wax. A string quartet's lilting melodies emanate from the chandeliers with the aroma of lavender.

I will lay down beside Bernadette and hold my cheek against hers. This simple contact fills my being with elation. Our lips meet and I stroke her hair, touch her skin turned a glowing pink. My own skin is tingling through excitement as I undress her – this mindroom is private, doctor. You'll have to stay outside for a while.

I'll sprinkle you with kisses, my palms tenderly moving over you before the union.

A delicious fragrance while me make love. I can believe in the divided soul of self for I'm split into two entities. It seems as if the effort required to leave my body and stand on the other side of the room as an observer wouldn't be much. Then the potential has passed, having been seduced to remain with the physical aspects of being. As I encircle, breathe you in and in, we blend; I see you made of glass. Melt into this sensual domain, a plunging communion as strong as prayer, speaking with fragrant spears and knowing you sweetly burn with my glorious burning; entangled within a secret paralysis while the moment revolves, evolves until the suspended empty space yields too soon, becoming the final surrender. Sensual peeling of skin, jolts of electric ecstasy, one after the other, time after time after time. And as you cry out a name, it's easily ignored as an unknown dialect, while I'm ripped apart like a tissue, an escape from mind to body that has been captured, concentrated and released.

I'm energized. I have repaired. A religious revelation could never compare. Cast up onto the beach of sublime lethargy while I'm left simply holding you, both of us silent.

We belong to each other, the crucial and elemental parts having become inseparable, moulded into a single entity. My treasure, you I worship, be with me forever.

Already the wax blocks are melting to reveal a key and a lock, one opening the other for the benefit of the rhapsody.

The true now. I have been flaming – able to steer destiny to avoid any obstacle, any tragedy – yes, here on the bed with my wife stretched out beside me, the summer held in an early evening. I only imagine sitting on a train, going somewhere alone and cold, an emptiness inside. And the repetitious clatter of wheels on the tracks, distracting buzz of voices. How quickly my Bernadette fades. As I open my eyes, I find that they're already open but somehow had been blinded. And there are those other eyes burrowing into me like jabbing rods.

'Are you listening?'

Clement focused. The woman before him had her legs crossed and arms severely folded. She had wrapped her cape back over her. Two young men and an older man dressed in a heavy overcoat had turned their attention to him. One of the men was smirking, the other curling his lip, the third appearing worried or serious.

'I said, are you listening to me?' the woman repeated.

'Pardon?' Clement was feeling disoriented as though he had been aroused from sleep. 'Apologies,' he replied above the train's rhythm, 'I wasn't aware you were talking.'

'Why do you keep on looking at me? Are you a pervert, dressed up like a clown gone wrong? Staring at me in that … way.' Saliva had caught in her throat and the last word had been spoken unnaturally.

'Come out of your coma, have you?' snapped one of the young men from the other side of the compartment. He turned to the woman. 'If you need any help, give me a shout. And as for you,' he continued, waving a finger at Clement, 'you definitely need expert help. You'd better get out at the next station or I'll call a guard. Then you'll be in a lot of trouble, believe me.'

'No really, don't worry about it,' the woman replied, clutching at her cape.

Clement began to explain to the distressed woman. 'This fine lady is right. I was reconstructing inside, you see.' She looked quickly away. 'If viewpoint is turned inward I can live in all sorts of wonderful rooms. I may have been looking but not seeing anything of your being.' Clement had been gesticulating with twirls of his arm to emphasise his sentences. The woman seemed not to be listening. She held her attention to the carriage window, her lips pressed firmly together. 'Excuse me?' Clement added to attract her attention.

'Listen,' barked the older man, 'leave her alone, I'm warning you.'

Clement began to laugh, cracks appearing in the foundation make-up on his slim face. The situation had become amusing. Before him sat a person who had pretended to be Bernadette, who had somehow stolen her face for a while until he had seen through it for the mask it was. Who had demanded he listen to her; who, when he had attempted to reply in a civil manner, had ignored him. And there over in the corner (which had darkened as the train passed through another cutting,) was a man threatening him for no apparent reason. A man with a ridiculous hat perched upon a squashed melon of a head. And that melon, wrinkled and yellow with plastic features pinned to it – a goatee beard here, bulging eyes there, with a grape of a nose and a mouth expression which defied description.

12

Clement had moved to another compartment of the carriage and stood rocking with the movements of it. The constant rhythms of train wheels on the tracks were making his weariness worse. Monotonous hammering set up monotonous couplets. He began to put words to these metres which he found difficult to shift: 'Where are we going, the land of the Minerva; where are we going, the land of the Ra…'

No sooner had he managed to exterminate one quatrain, another would be born with the same insistent stubbornness: 'Shouldn't do that, it'll cost you a lot, shouldn't do that, it's all that I've got…'

He licked the end of a finger and touched both eyelids with it. A concerted mental effort was needed to stay awake.

He began to clear his throat but then the owner of a brown coat who leant by the train doors let out a gruff cough.

No wonder this peculiar man barked – he has the features of a bloodhound; loose skin about his lazy face, dozy eyes sunken in their orbits. Over on the other side, a snuffling badger with a plastered thumb, opening his jaws. And sitting beside him with the clever watch, a lizard, scratching with scaled boney fingers.

Clement wondered what sort of creations they were, these everyday commuters posing as a menagerie of animals with their skin no doubt made of a clever plastic. Covering an ingenious flexible alloy, able to be transformed at the will of the bodies' inhabitants; a metamorphosis into any animal they wished to be.

Insignificant elements caught his attention. A passenger possessed the nose of a hog, overlarge with a bulbous, reddish end and grimy pores covering its length. This fleshy protuberance seemed farcical, jutting out rudely from its unshaven face.

A youth in one of the carriage corners had a sharp beak of a nose. The lanky bird-youth rummaged in a plastic bag and extracted a sandwich as delicately as if handling fine porcelain. The triangles of bread were moving unhurriedly from lap to mouth as he returned an empty stare.

A woman leant into the aisle from the next compartment showing her rotund face, bearing a resemblance to a grinning cat.

But not cats. Out of the way! Get out of my rooms. Don't, no. Did it experience its own beatific madness? Mustn't think on.

Who's controlling these room filmics anyway? Look at noses again, at beaks, at muzzles and snouts; count the vibrating stripes, just yellow ones. How dare it present such an ugly performance from its pitiful torment.

Look out of the autumn-smudged window, that's the answer; see slabs of concrete and dead trees … the flash of contents in this sealed mindroom again.

And yet, I must try to face up to these as you insist, doctor. But only a few. I'll choose a different route; the car ahead should do the same. Purple car between street lamps; the next pool of light will change you to magenta and I'll be framing the cameo horror with my car headlamps.

The cat darting from the safety of a garden. Run faster, run – you are hesitating, body flinching but not into motion. Almond eyes reflecting the lights as flame … flash, fast … not fast enough: paw with the weight of the car ahead upon it. Claws splintering, leg bone snapping, wrenching muscle and twisting flesh. Cease this ugly blasphemy. No animal should be allowed to act so absurdly as it spits and leaps in spasms, painting the tarmac with black blood. Why should it grin like a crazy bloodied toy as it rolls in ecstatic frenzy? Watch the contortions, the cat snapping at pain in the mangled leg, trauma jerking its body. Mindless in agony, it's performing the writhing ballet of the senseless, squirming and flexing like a snake.

Get out of the car to calm it.

Whites of its eyes. Hissing from its twitching form. I must

get to a vet before it's too late. Soothe it with comforting words, explain painkillers and splints, antibiotics and recuperation. But how can it understand? To be in torment with something which you have no way of comprehending is a thousand-fold magnified.

The cat-woman's sibilance: her words formed tangles of ectoplasmic string which writhed above the passengers. They became entangled in a luggage rack then snagged on a crossword-puzzler's poised pen before seeping surreptitiously through the seam between the carriage doors.

Clement was proud of this new skill. A dog-man replied to the cat-woman with a stutter of a laugh, each separate emission plump and gong-like. Whispers, Clement evaluated at once, were umber strips covered in fur; bloodied glass-like shards would be manifestations of a scream, sinuous aromatic honey, the ultimate moans of orgasm.

He guessed what Dr Leibkov was thinking. Such a doubting man, unwilling to stretch limits of his professional knowledge with a reticence to explore unfamiliar territory. That individual was trapped as surely as a beetle in a matchbox. If only Clement could somehow show the doctor that four dimensions are ephemeral and as easy to remove as the three dimensions of old wallpaper. Then he could unveil the more valid world hidden beneath. Even point the way for him to capture an essence of abstruse spaces between thoughts.

His attention was taken again by the bird-youth who had

eaten a sandwich. He fiddled with controls of a music player. Tinny notes were heard from the earphones, interrupted by whistling oscillations. A couple sitting opposite the young man were becoming over-generous with their glances. They seemed agitated and uncomfortable and they slowly turned to each other. This duo of slothful movers with their lingering looks could be connected together somehow, Clement thought, maybe by invisible cables.

A regimental-looking man began to tap the metal ferrule of his umbrella onto the carriage floor. It made a dry knocking, adding to the consistent pulse of the train wheels. The howlings, whistles and drumbeats increased as the owner of the digital device turned up the volume.

Stop immediately – Clement wanted to warn him – before you scratch the hidden scheme further!

You've already scored cuts, slashed at complex virtual structures. Defiled them with your black box as it sends out magnetic impulses laced with battalions of viciously serrated wheels. A barbaric invention, slashing at the mindrooms.

But these mechanical companions, trapped as they are, couldn't begin to comprehend.

I have talents far superior to any of you. I can sense time as a living dimension, a malleable clay which I'll soon be able to refashion. I can see the very substance of sounds. I can take my inner being out of this fleshy apparel of mine; I'm able to temporarily escape the confines of physical self.

There, way beyond the solidified liquid of the window, through those quiet, leafless trees – woodsmoke. A flaring of yellow, crackling of branches eaten by the flames. I am that man dressed in a black overcoat and boots, poking the fire with a bark-stripped stick. I'll watch the glowing inner sanctum within. I need to step back from the stinging batches of smoke.

Another element: inhuman screams through the winter-defiled woodland, horrors on its heels, running for sanctuary to my ears. A badger is struggling to free itself, preparing to gnaw flesh away and bite through the bone of its own leg to escape metal teeth embedded there. But it's useless to struggle. Each convulsive movement produces an excruciating pain. Someone has to help, to free me from this torture. You there, wizened woman, collecting wood for your hearth. Though I've turned down my hearing aid to stop illicit sound shapes from desecrating the transparent silk of the wind. A snake of a train is weaving past, up on the embankment. I wave to the imposters on their way to the city.

I'll wave back, though this train has already left the veteran housekeeper behind in her ravaged woods.

Now featureless office buildings and anonymous blocks of flats. Why has the train stopped on this pretend bridge? I'm already late. My legs are aching.

Car after car, interspersed with vans and thundering lorries, being swallowed up beneath us, all with roaring engines. The growling one, must have a hole in the exhaust box. Sounding like a helicopter.

Or a motor boat. I spy both here. Whirring helicopters hovering like metal insects. The speedboats pulling waterskiers over by The Neptune Hotel.

I'll watch the merry-go-round spin with its twisted poles, each impaling a wild-maned horse, ridden by children sending out peals of laughter to mingle with pipe organ music emanating like copper stick insects. And adults with strained smiles upon their sunburned faces, stiffly posed upon their wooden mounts. Attempting to retain dignity, pretending they're not enjoying the juvenile delight of their rotating journey to the end of nowhere. I can read, through the cafeteria windows, the ornate lettering around the top of the ride as it spins: Colonel Hiprod's Thrilling Horses. Here, doctor, I can imagine the merry-go-round sheering from its greasy hub and gently spinning above the sea to the beach, casting a black plate of a shadow over the stunned tourists. A craftily disguised time machine, able to preserve those thrilling minutes, to set them within amber.

Time can be deceiving and wicked though. A deception, I might add, whose pigeon-hole is next to your trickery, Dr Leibkov. You shamelessly promote an ugly form of salvation. Time promises eternity to the young. If she is mounted upon a horse, then the animal walks leisurely beside you in your infancy. She murmurs oaths and pledges of the most attractive kind. But taken over by the spell you're not aware she's shaken the reins. Her horse is trotting. You're matching the pace to catch any precious jewels she gives. And as you marvel in this supposed immortal place, her piebald mare breaks into a canter. 'Wait for me,' is your plea and you start to run. She throws pouches of joy and trinkets of sensation, occasionally spiked metal balls of pain. But we run faster when she lets out showers of experience. The steed is galloping and you find the brute not so high – you've grown taller. You have been fooled by this robed siren. She has you in her firm grasp, holding you to the sweating horse's side. You feel your muscles shrivelling and teeth dropping, bones becoming brittle. Skin drying like parchment, a network of wrinkles like baked mud. And you cry with an imploring shriek, 'Not so fast!' with fingers set like eagle's claws, gripping the mane. You look back. There's your life given in trinkets, pouches, on plinths, in glass, littering the road. She whips the rippling muscles and digs spurs into the bolting animal. 'Slow down,' you are pleading. 'Give me time to repair and replay.' But for guilty ones there's only a shuddering, mournful wail. They are jerked out of this bad dream life and plunged into the unknown landscape beyond one of the ultimate barriers. And the deceiving one has no place in this timeless void. She goes back to lure others away from the repairing.

See a man walking without vitality. Creeping along with leaden steps, bent over with an invisible load. His fingers look like white roots. He says, 'Cold, so cold.' He looms larger than most, wearing many coats. The edges overlap like the rings of a tree stump, forming a multi-toned stratum. He appears to be walking across the surface of an ocean made of coins.

And there's another in torment. The woman is holding palms out towards the furling waves. The waves rattle and chink onto pebbles. She's unable to capture even one coin. Bitter tears blind her to a writhing figure. But he has no time for her outpourings of sorrow. Hear him gnashing hidden teeth as he tumbles above the clanking waters, his laughable member proud from between his thighs. He has no hands or feet. His twisted mouth has been sealed, all bodily orifices grown over with thick plugs of flesh. Agonized eyes screwed tightly shut with his tortuous frustrations.

A choir of gulls have surrounded another. Their cries have become beautiful voices. The man throws down his notebook and presses palms of his hands onto his ears. He shouts a raucous, idiotic jumble in an attempt to drown the sweet sounds. He refuses to listen to this exquisite accomplishment, running about, slapping the birds, imploring them to stop. Ripping the wings from one, punching another in mid-flight. A crow has added a baritone. It flies in ever decreasing circles until it finally comes to rest on the light fitting hanging on chains from the ceiling.

Harold is holding a white cup to his lips. I'll let you hide still, doctor.

'Extraordinary. Then what happened?'

'Freddie suggests we get a ladder from the printshop. But then the frightened bird defecates again and the product showers onto the accounts office carpet like a white distemper. Sarah is coming through the other doorway, holding a bucket.

I guess her idea is to place it on the floor in direct line with the tail feathers. Freddie is poking that shivering crow with the brush end of a broom. It flies off again with a cawing, dislodging dust from its illuminated perch. We're at a loss what to do, bumping into each other or the desks, knocking over baskets.

'We're rendered immobile by the arrival of Stones. The only sounds are from the beating wings of the trapped creature.

'There are five birds, now ten. Twenty or thirty, maybe more; like black bats, like haunted umbrellas swooping and floating. I could have them attack Stones if I want.

'He stares at the defiled carpet, to the dust and muck spattered over papers and keyboards.

'Finch tells him about the proofreader's window left open over the weekend. I'm in for it.

'Here I am, back in his office, Stones reprimanding: 'You've failed me, Penshart Press and yourself,' banging a palm on the desk, ramping his anger. He insinuates my salary review next month won't happen.'

'It does seem he over-reacted. What did you say then?'

What I could have said. Cover your ears, Harold; I don't want you thinking less of me.

You're an overblown, hollow bag, Stones, squandering my talents, paying me a pittance. You destroy mindrooms, damage the barriers. I want to tell you where you can stuff your pathetic job—'

'Have you told Bernadette?'

'No, I haven't, to be honest.'

Harold always appears worried in this mindroom. He's letting his sight fall into the cup of coffee before him then over to me, to gauge my expression. 'Donald, if you need financial help, just say. Bernadette is used to a certain standard of living. There's not much worse than money troubles. I should know. Before I was married...'

I'll switch off, just watch his lips open and close, fish-like; see his hand gesticulate before going back to his pipe as though the charred wooden bowl needs touches of reassurance. Notice his pate shining as if glazed with varnish, reflecting the lemon glare of the cafeteria lights. Becoming silent after a while, waiting for an answer. 'Yes, I understand,' I reply. This seems to satisfy him.

We sip our beverages. Clammy and airless in here. Dejected waitresses wander aimlessly between the benches and tables, scooping up paper plates or crackling cellophane. There's the occasional clatter of crockery and hiss of fat from the hot plates.

Doctor, let me describe: the cafeteria is lined with full-length windows on two sides though the sun prefers to shun the interior. The bright deck of the pier with its railings and the glittering band of sea form a mural over the large transparent panes. And it's only the intermittent sight of a tourist strolling by or one of the pennants giving a limp wave which destroys the deception. A gull screeches, sounding like a hideous laugh.

A match flares as Harold prepares to light his pipe. I can feel him looking at me still.

'I'm not one to pry, as well you know, Donald. But if you have problems then speak out. We can't have standards falling, can we?'

'Thank you, Harold, though nothing that can't be sorted.'

'I'll be brutally honest; you seem a bit of a dreamer. Bernadette is unsure of herself. I would ask you become a little stronger. Show her the way.'

'But I think I do.'

'Give her the confidence she lacks.' He's pausing to comply with his smoker's cough.

That gives me the opportunity to interrupt. 'Time we met the girls.'

The octopus machine over in the funfair is paddling into movement. 'Precisely.'

'I don't see what you mean.'

'Up and down, round and around, that's precisely the reason why I don't want to go on it. I'd spew.'

'Donald, be quiet. I don't think we want to hear.' I have just noticed freckles on Bernadette's nose.

'It'll splatter everywhere,' answers Marianne.

'Really sis, you're as bad as him.'

We're walking hand in hand past the Ferris wheel. Marianne and Harold follow us ten paces behind. They've stopped by another souvenir shop window at the display of conch shells, lighthouse ashtrays, lumps of quartz or polished pebbles, sugar sticks and peppermint pigs.

Din of funfair activity. The drone of fairground motors is camouflaged by music crackling from speakers. Over there, those bumper cars zipping around their neutral course, each one skewered with a pole ending with a flexed strip of metal, rattling and showering sparks from the grid above. A dry odour of oily graphite lingers, strong enough to vanquish the smell of doughnuts, hamburgers and the hotdogs. More frenetic noises and lights from the amusement arcades.

'You've done it. I didn't know you could shoot.'

'Binny, what do you mean? Expert I am. Actually it's quite easy.'

'I guess that. But easy for you? Not very good with your hands, are you? Admit it. When it comes down to practical things you're slow on the uptake.'

'Really don't know what you're on about. It's just a daft duck shoot.' Her bluff attitude is annoying me.

Marianne and her father have caught up.

'You two arguing?' Marianne in a playful mood.

I'll replace the rifle to the counter. The security chain rattles and sweeps the spare pellets to the slats, already strewn with cigarette butts and cartons. Under our feet, the sea moving forever.

'No argument, just saying. You know Donald. He has trouble wiring a plug, let alone shooting metal ducks.'

There's happy laughter coming from the beach where a Punch and Judy show stands with its back to the waves, trapped by clusters of delighted onlookers and striped deckchairs. Why stripes? They don't have to be. I find it a detestable pattern.

At the entrance of the arcade with its crazy flashing lights, the bleach-faced sailor dummy balancing on the barrel of rum within its glass box. That inane inebriated humour about its lips, those vacuous eyes, hands like paddles held to its belly.

'I've run out of change.'

A moment later and Marianne has put a silver coin into the slot. Immediately the peculiar figure begins to jiggle and wobble on the barrel, giving its insane laughter to its amused audience.

I'll place it at the end of the pier, where the white chalet used to stand.

'Anyone want seafood?' Harold asks.

I'll sprinkle the small pot of cockles with pepper and douse them in vinegar. On the stall, a dead crab in its bed of ice, holding its pincers up like castanets. Eels writhe in a tangle in their tub next to piles of whiskered shrimps. Bernadette and Marianne prod at whelks with their plastic forks. A seagull is standing on the roof of the arcade watching us. Harold has his back to the dancing lights of the arcade machines.

You see how cheerful we are, doctor! A quality mindroom on the pier, filled with positive waves.

'Who's coming on the ghost train with me?'
Marianne grinning. 'I will.'

13

As we thud through these rubber doors in our small open ride, the squalling funfair awash in sunshine is lost, replaced with blackness and dank coldness. Stale, but I find it refreshing after the sun washing my face with sweat. Now we're bathed in phosphorescent lights. And from one of the alcoves at the side, a skeleton descends close to shrieking girls in the ride behind. Marianne is laughing. A moan of a comically ghoulish nature emanates from around this tunnel. My face is brushed with slippery lengths of string hanging down from amongst the severed anatomical pieces swinging above. A headless phantom floats in front of the first ride before disappearing into a blood-spattered wall. Other alcoves light up, showing horror maquettes or glowing spiders.

Marianne exclaiming above the grinding wheels and the sound effects: 'This is fun.'

A door is swinging open and a figure bound in bandages lurches out. Marianne shrinks into her seat as he lumbers towards her but our clanking ride judders past the monster in the neon-lit tunnel with an accompaniment of slicing axes.

We've turned another corner into a small area, lit only by a single red bulb. The rides have stopped. With the compliment of a hacking, evil laugh, an eight-foot giant has stepped out. The floor is covered with boulders made of balsa wood. There's rubber snakes squirming, and dismembered lumps of polystyrene flesh.

A hush as wolves cease their howling. We must listen to this giant. The urgent whispers from the other passengers are fading as a bellowing emits from between the giant's cracked lips.

'Welcome to my new world where anything is possible.' He has straggling lengths of hair and a beard, and round, penetrating eyes. He sways in his boots as if on a train. His face though, I've recognized it. He's the old man of the sea. Sure enough there's a crate – poking out from behind one of those slashed curtains covering a wardrobe – containing pint bottles of brown ale, catching this torrid red light which stains us all. 'Applaud the battle of Evermore by the mountains of madness. If you wish to view the treasures of Atlantis then come with me. See them swaddled in their caverns of splendour with stalactites of precious metals and stalagmites of diamond. Join a band of gypsies with their caravan of camels. Or maybe burrow into the earth – more than nine feet underground – to sink past layers of history. Through magma chambers roaring with rivers of lava until we reach the sepulchre core. Perhaps your desire is to discover mysteries of the universe: astronomy domine. Only I have been granted the revered task of showing the chosen ones such cosmic marvels. We shall travel across to the other side via unimaginably vast tracts of negative reality, transfused by galaxies and nebulae. Pass Jupiter and Saturn, Neptune, Titan, frightening stars, steering around howling meteor storms. Acknowledge solar systems, recognize crucial planetary orbits; voyage beyond the most distant constellation. There you will see a black hole extending far out to the left and right, the great divide. You must understand, Mrs Froby is correct in what she implies: infinity is not a number but a state. We shall plunge into this ungraspable, timeless nothingness, this space oddity. And there will be the secrets incarcerated within giant edifices, like fortresses, like barriers. Each different, reflecting a little of what they contain. Some are able to dazzle you with their intense brightness. Others are as smooth as milk – unscalable, impregnable. While still more are alive with locket-shaped fans which must always be in constant movement, teasing you by showing glimpses between their agitation. Then there are those which have been armoured with fortified metals. And these barriers have to be broken into for them to expose arcane labyrinths of wonderment. There is no other way. Raze them to the ground, annihilate them to uncover truths which lay dormant inside.'

I have leapt out of the ghost train ride. Marianne, swirling concern on your pert face I can understand.

'You must get out, all of you, away from this mockery, this

sham. You're an impostor, a charlatan!' Already the linked rides have rattled off, leaving me and the giant only. I'll expose this scoundrel who pretends to offer enlightenment.

I'm correct in my assumptions. No gentle giant here. Close up I see that the high boots are short stilts. He's unstrapping them and kicked one of the rocks. Sure enough this is not a cleverly painted piece of balsa wood but real rock. A snake hisses and its spiked tongue flickers before slithering into shadow. I daren't inspect the flesh.

His face – the visage of an intrepid sailor – even this is a lie. I'll pull down the mask, rip it away to expose your real identity, as if I didn't already know.

There you are, hiding behind your disguise. You must understand, Dr Leibkov, it's a difficult undertaking to fool me. You might as well be in a glass house. As if you could show me a saucerful of secrets! I already have inklings of what they are. I can penetrate through the mere external steel covering of the replacements. I've the ability to look at sounds, to explain and explore their solidifying shapes. I can manipulate time within multiple dimensions. You must appreciate how honoured I am to have been bestowed such astonishing abilities. They will hold me in good stead for cryptic enigmas which I'll eventually uncover by myself. The patterns this train makes, for instance. Can you interpret them? I have my doubts. But still you've the gall to say you can help.

Although I detect – sometimes – there's something wrong. But the problem's elusive. I'm led into mental dead ends. I feel like a turkey with its innards scraped out, all of me frozen and wrapped in a tight, airless prison of cling film. I can see about but can't seem to communicate through this all-encompassing mantle. Am I making sense, doctor? It frightens me sometimes. There's a hateful barrier between us as though we've placed a sheet of glass there looking like a train window.

'You're making sense, Donald. You are lucid again, able to tell me your worries. That is good. It's at times like this when you are able to vocalise your condition in a coherent manner. You must appreciate – and take courage – eventually you will be as you are today, all of the time. It will be as though a curtain has been taken away. Your mind will be cleansed of its muddy thoughts.'

'Yes, that's it. Muddy thoughts. Though some of them have barbs; or they can burn as if with a caustic substance — getting a bit far-fetched again, aren't I? What I mean is, those mindrooms seeming not part of me, created despite myself, they can hurt.'

'Perhaps in not knowing.'

'Fabled loss of yesterday's dreams?'

'Can you think of any of those hurtful mindrooms, Donald?'

'Doctor, don't make me do that. I can't, I won't.'

'Soon you will be able to. We will sort your concerns together. It's going to be a long haul up a steep hill but it will be done.'

'Or through a train tunnel.'

'As you wish. The light at the end is imperceptible at the moment but will be there soon, rest assured. I will remind you again: if you have any troubles, you are at liberty to ring me day or night. Don't bottle it until the next session.'

'You are a wise man, doctor. I have complete faith in your judgement.'

'Excellent. In that case, you must heed my words. These mental barriers are particularly strong. We must try to break them down to ascertain what hides behind. That must be confronted. There are those who are as sensitive, fragile plants, too easily crushed. I suspect you are one of these people, Donald. Because of a natural sensitivity we will take the process slowly and with care.'

'Sort of undiluted mindroom filmics, isn't it, Dr Leibkov?'

'Yes, harsh memories which you must eventually face. Now, Donald, I wish to ask you a question. I'm interested, that's all. Why do you call me Dr Leibkov?'

Gently down the stream…

'Are you trying to frighten me? You are – you're my doctor.'

'Calm yourself. I am Dr Smythe. My real name which you have called me up until yesterday. Does changing my name have something to do with your cocoon experiments?'

'Rather surprised the government should clamp down in this way, allowing you only verbal weapons to attack the general public. In league with you, aren't they, for funded gadgets to pump me full of bad waves. Though with the way I'm feeling at the moment, I believe you've somehow managed already. Drilled with a computer web, did you, to give me your treatment? You think you can unwrap me as easily as a parcel. That's what you do, I know. No use denying it. Buzzing boxes as well, with needles and long prodding poles. Because everybody knows you can treat us as though we were animals in a slaughter house, herded into this pen. Those dressed for work: reading, sleeping, talking contentedly, unaware of their true destination. Have we not hurtled passed two stations already without stopping?

'Am I the only one to perceive the truth? We must systemize our linkages before it's too late.

'All real people must be told. Every action overlaps. If one element isn't there, like depriving a clock of its fly wheel, how can you expect it to run? From the smallest eyebrow twitch to the largest sets of activities in a lifetime, everything is equal.

'Things affect all other things in a complicated away. If elements in space and time are bonded so strongly, if by changing one small event influences so much, then why couldn't this be controlled for one's own purpose? Like removing pebbles from a garden. By the placement of elastic bands of eternity. By time dilation, squeezing and stretching seconds and minutes for particular usages. Simple causes produce complicated effects. Like an uncountable series of binary switches clicking off and on round the globe, one action affecting the next into another action, and so on. What type of rings radiate?

Sorcerers transmuted metals – lead to gold – or banished

evil and disease by the same principles of element timing and juxtaposition. Though these enlightened ones were swept aside as deluded. Yet these practitioners were the scientists of their time.

'So now you've discovered the cocoon experiment is not totally mine. It's a modern extension of the work by those who have gone before.'

'Would you like me to be honest, Donald?'

'Of course. Anything else would be futile, surely?'

'Yes it would. You mind is disturbed; you have admitted already. We are attempting to unclutter, take away thoughts which don't belong, those which can only lead to confusion and distress. I find your theories interesting and imaginative but more importantly, they are misguided. You feel you need such ideas despite them being destructive. Tell me, Donald, what do you hope to achieve with these experiments?'

'Why do my questions always beg another from you? Are you a government spy? If I can't trust you then who can I trust? You're no better than the mechanoid kid with his crackling music player and mushy sandwiches. Or those machines pretending ladies stuttering in whispers, no doubt discussing me.

The electronic android tapping the end of its umbrella, it has a familiar rhythm to it. Morse code. Craftily passing on a message.

'What – dashes, dots – do – you – more dots, dashes – hope, to, achieve – dots and dashes – from – your – dots bloody dashes – experiments. You never give up, do you? Your sort have snoopers everywhere, a treacherous network under control.

'If you really must know, I'm on the way to discover the exact configuration. This'll create the enchanting mouth to kiss, face to caress, soft hair to stroke. The woman who is indestructible, able to resist flames, whose perfection was compromised but who can be repaired. The special someone to love again in a future perfect mindroom. My Bernadette.'

14

'**R**eclaim our joy, peace and happiness. Become a family of two once more. That's important, I know. And I do love kids, before you ask again. They're the innocence before defilement, the soiling of adulthood, infinite stasis broken, blessings forgotten. But that's not what I'm saying. You twist everything to your own advantage.'

'You promised though. How could you go against your promise?' Those bright lanterns sway gently in the breeze blowing in from the darkened sea. Far off, the lights of a ship. 'Donald, why aren't you answering?'

'Look, let me get you another drink.' I'll reach out to take her glass. She's pulled it away.

'I don't want that. I want an answer.' She stares, fixed to me, as though this might anchor me there.

I'm turning to lean on the railing, the black waters slopping against the walls of the jetty. Ghosts of boats bob in the harbour. Vague white spots are the gulls nesting in the cliffs over to the west. Laughter has come from the bar. I can feel

Bernadette's critical observation still upon me.

'Let me get myself a drink then. We can talk about it after, in a much better mindroom.'

Turning back for a moment to see the clean moon shining in her hair and highlighting couples and groups.

A parent is attempting to keep her child under control, luring him away from the willow trees lit by lanterns. 'Jonathan, get away.'

There, doctor, the silhouette of Bernadette, indicating for him to go back to his concerned mother.

Three friends are standing equidistantly around the perimeter of the fountain base, its lamps shining from beneath the shallow water. There's a colour for each of them, making one red as though he's by a camp fire, the second a ghoulish green and the third turned yellow. It's Green who speaks. 'A pint in it for you.' The concrete dolphin – its tail merging with the plinth – suddenly has spurted a cascade from its mouth. It's made the surface of the water in the base alive with tinkling droplets. Yellow is finding this extremely funny. 'Beat me to it!' he says to Green. I still don't know what he means.

Ivy, studded with lightbulbs, covers the wall and parts of the large gold letters spelling the name "The Neptune Hotel". Tucked into a corner, not far from double doors leading to the main bar, a couple sit on a bench in the shadows, clutching each other.

Delete them. Good, the bench is empty. The last time I'll have to do that. Those three about the fountain will act as guardians, to make sure no one else ever sits there. Easily done.

The same shrill mother from the beer garden. 'Johnny, if you don't come here this instant…' The little fellow has run back to his new friend. A shadow-play set on the end of the jetty. The black background has been dabbed with white dots to represent stars. Yellow has been sprayed to make a moon with moonlight hints on the edges of silk clouds. The shape of railings has been cut out of cardboard and laid below it. Then two figures, life-like and sharply defined, are placed: one delineating the cut-out of Bernadette, bending from the waist, the other, the boy.

I'll squeeze between these two sofas, nodding from one drink to the other in my hands.

'There we go.' I'll put them on the copper topped table and sit.

'What's this?'

'What do you mean? Vodka and orange. That's what you wanted in this mindroom. I've also created a circle of metal trees around us.'

'Donald, I asked for Martini and lemonade.'

'Oh, I'd swear you…' I should stand again to change it but Bernadette has hold of my sleeve.

'Doesn't matter, this'll do.'

We're sitting next to the figurehead. I'll rub a palm over its roughened surface. 'He must have seen a lot, do you reckon?'

She's not paying attention. Her sight is towards the wall of engravings and prints. Men are there with casual stances, holding pint jugs and tankards, chatting in groups of three and four. They are the shopkeepers from the mall and the pier attendants, I think.

'Who you staring at?'

'No one. Carry on.'

'I was saying, this figurehead … Bernadette, what are you playing at?'

'Nothing. It's just that — forget it.'

'How am I expected to, when you purposefully aren't attempting to change your memory? When you've opened the wrong mindroom again?'

'Me?' She's leaning forward to speak in a whisper. 'Alright, don't look, but the man in the striped jacket.' But I can't resist the temptation. I'll turn around casually as I always do, eyes sweeping the room. 'I told you, don't look. Ooh, you can be embarrassing sometimes.' She's slapped the back of my hand resting on the table.

I've spotted him. I try my hardest to change what I see, every time. But no, he's always there in that bright summer jacket with its red, white and black stripes. It stands out from amidst the blues and browns. He brings his glass to his lips. Taking it away again, leaving froth on his black moustache which he then wipes with his bottom lip. He looks to me. Or rather past me. And he makes a subtle but definite gesture with the fingers on his left hand as though it might be a secret sign. Perhaps my imagination overtakes at this point. All the same,

I whip around to face Bernadette; catch whatever reaction I might find.

'Didn't I tell you?' She comments before smiling and nodding over my shoulder.

'What are you doing? Who is he?'

Though I know, the name burned away. This mindroom will soon be repaired. Surely, it must.

'Last week, on the pier.'

'When last week? You never told me. Who is this bloke? Tell me quickly, then I won't tell the doctor. It can't be Aaron. He's rotting in the harbour.'

'For goodness sake, Donald, stop getting worked up. When you were with Marianne on the ghost train.'

'Is this the truth?"

Bernadette's lips tighten, I always see that. She's blurting, 'Alright, if you must know, it was when you forgot to pick me up the week before last.' I'm becoming annoyed. She continues in a lighter tone, 'He's a palm reader. Reads tarot cards as well, from a little white chalet at the end of the pier. Only a temporary job, though.'

'Oh I see, got chatting, did we, to a figment of your imagination?'

'Really, Donald, you're getting me nettled. Wasn't expensive if you're worried.'

'That's not it.' How can I explain without sounding foolish the idea of anyone else touching even your hand ties a knot in me? 'Alright, what did he have to say before he drowned?'

'I'm going to have a happy life. There are going to be changes.'

'What sort of changes?'

'Three children; the usual stuff. Live to a ripe old age. And when—'

'All hogwash you know.'

'I haven't said any different, have I? But the bit about the children.' She's squeezing my hand.

'Hot in here. I'm going to have a nose around the beer garden, see if the other mindroom has improved.'

I notice she's disappointed because I've changed the subject. 'If you want,' she answers, shrugging. She's picking up her drink, and as I walk away, her eyes are seeking his again.

Let his top half slip from the bottom half, slop to the floor, pint of beer emptying over the feet of the others. He doesn't deserve a uniting elastic band.

The guardians by the fountain still stand immobile, protective, vigilant. Just as they should be. I'll stroll across the grass between the willow trees and picnic benches, over to Bernadette who's leaning on the railing. Put my pint of ale down on the concrete base of the rails. I'll slip my hands onto her waist and hold her to me. But there's no response. She might as well be a mannequin. Still she stares out to a blacker, shifting sea as if searching for someone. I've realized she's crying. I'll gently take her by the shoulders. Her long hair, still with the moon tinting it, has fallen over her white face.

Lantern light highlights her tears.

'Hey, Binny, shh, what is it?'

'You know what.' Always whimpers. Always turns her back.

'Listen, you know we can't afford it. I'd love a family as much as you but not at the moment. We struggle with the mortgage every month as it is. Just wouldn't be practical, would it? Let's wait another year at least. There's no rush. A year's no time, you'll see.'

She doesn't reply. The gold locket glitters from the night lights. Is it green? Still gold.

Finally, she speaks. 'Alright, no babies then.'

'That's right. I'm glad you see sense.'

'Then I want to go out to work.'

'You must be joking. My wife working? No way. You shouldn't have to. The husband works and the wife stays at home.'

'And looks after the children.'

'Very clever. Not what I meant.'

'Oh, I know it's not what you meant.' Spinning around to glare at me. 'You've got it every way, haven't you?'

'Don't know what you mean.'

'We can't afford to have a baby but you won't let me bring in a bit of money so we can. A part-time job.'

'Like doing what?'

'I don't know. You make it seem uncommon. Millions of women work. Anyone would think you're Victorian. Secretarial temping work like when I met you; barmaid…'

'Oh no you don't.'

She's obviously annoyed. 'You can't tell me what to do. We may be married, but it doesn't mean I have to obey what you say.'

'So you didn't mean what you said in church — Binny, come back...'

She's marching away in the direction of the fountain guardians. Keep away from the bench, go anywhere but there. Better still, return. I didn't mean what I had babbled. Let's have a bubble-blowing infant to share. Come here, I can change. Not too late, is it? Doctor, does it have to be how I fear it might? I can alter the past which will be the future, believe me. Here, as I watch green-black water slurping and slapping below; look, over there ... there, floating just under the surface: bloated form, hair moving like a fine sea plant, flesh turned to green sponge, a white pastry; those empty sockets, the crabs from inside of the skull via the gaping mouth. See how I can show truth, here at my feet. All that's left of Aaron, the crap palm reader. I can be believed. I want us to have a baby. Are you listening?

15

'**B**ernadette?'

'What? I was about to fall asleep then. You've spoilt it. It's going to take me ages.' Mumbling into her pillow.

'Sorry.'

'You're always sorry. Keep quiet and goodnight.'

I'll touch her on the shoulder blade. She's shrugged me away with a flinch of her body. 'Go to sleep.'

'Let's make love,' I say hurriedly. 'Let me make love to you. Ten weeks, since the last time.' I'm whining but can't help myself. She stays silent. 'Bernadette, Binny – I love you.'

There was the time when these words held within them a myriad of songs, when it encompassed the universe, was as warm as a log fire. But now its icicle form betrays it for its true meaning of do you love me?

'Let me rest.' She's listless as sleep begins to tug, begins to take her away.

'A cuddle then.' I'm snuggling up to her back, stroking the embroidery of her nightgown. But she's wriggled and twisted quickly before sitting up. Her hair is dishevelled as she sways with tiredness.

'For goodness sake, Donald. I don't want a cuddle. I just want to sleep. Leave me alone.'

She slaps her head back down and it's buried into the pillow. The bed rises and falls for a second. Feeling hurt I'll turn my back on her and assume a similar position. Pull the eiderdown up to my neck. My whole being is yearning for her. I'm burning and wounded, and in no mood to sleep. There's slow breathing behind me.

Drumming of wheels as this trick train rumbles on. The scenery running past the windows, an extended piece of canvas dabbed expertly with pigment mixed with linseed oil. The noises made by the mock train, a clever recording. There might be a gang who've been employed to push and pull the carriages to simulate motion. But for what purpose? What is the motive? If I had the inclination, I'd leap out and tear down the canvas to see where we really are. I'll look back to the carriages and there − where the wheels should be − will be wooden blocks, and the passengers decorated dummies, their cogs scattered on the ground.

But how clever it is. Quite admirable really. The whole scene whistling by, the painting succeeding in making it appear so real, so convincingly 3D. A masterpiece of deception. The depth of field created in the town over there, sprawled like a slumbering beast, is exceptional; the occasional bursts of cold sunlight bouncing from office windows like a photographer's flashbulb firing is well done. And the stark buildings and pylons and telegraph poles.

Skimming past watch towers, water towers, house towers, vats and pipes and smoking cauldrons. There are oil drums, chimneys erect; a grassed field – a running man retrieving a stick while his panting dog looks on – under a bridge; rattling through a cutting, clattering past a station, plunging into another tunnel — these lights grow dim; they've gone out.

This thick blackness. A stifled coughing to a half moon.

'Are you awake?'

No reply except the ceasing of a rhythmic shuffling of bedclothes. I can feel my neck burn. Still she would rather enjoy herself than have me touch her. I will hold my breath but there's only silence. I'm going to pretend sleep. I'll make a convincing whistling through my teeth. It's not long before the regular shuffling begins again and I can feel the bed rocking gently. I'm stimulated and humiliated, interested yet enraged. Her breathing is becoming deeper but faster until it's a panting. The bed is creaking with the regular movement of her hands. Surely she must know I'm awake? She's letting out fleeting moans.

Breathing more rapidly with her, blood pumping in my throat. Faster she's going and the bed has set up a canter. The final energetic ruffling of the eiderdown and squeaking bed; a muffled whimper, then silence and stillness.

Had she known I'd been listening? I've been made to be excited and I want to touch myself. But sleep thunders up, presses down upon my eyelids, transports me away, past barren stretches, coal yards, motorways; watch towers, water towers, house towers.

The city maze. Look at it spread out, a rubbish dimension. Rambling mess of angular buildings and awkward traffic, interrupted by the dead river winding through it. Filthy sky fit for a filthy day.

I'll watch the landscape. See this symphony, as wretched and dreary as it is, with its rolling roads and legato parks, and cadences of decaying constructions. Always the same, scenes passing to be replaced with replicas, without a break.

Tattered corpse of a plastic bag flapping feebly, impaled by the twigs of a bush. It can flap as much as it likes, cry out if it wants. Won't make any difference to me.

Left behind, alone, the way it should be. Suffer alone otherwise it's a counterfeit suffering, a pretence. But then the lot is pretence anyhow.

Why should I care for anyone else's failings? They must solve their pathetic problems by themselves, doctor. Each person builds their own bridge like an artist does with a brush; the joining between their island and the outside world. Become aware of the inner self communicating to the outer one. I distinctly remember telling you this. But answer me: why is the outside world insisting on being the only true place?

Why shouldn't there be some other materiality, a difficult-to-get-at, hard-won reality made inside our own heads?

Certainly a subject we need to discuss more. And don't think I'm going to hide my annoyance when you'll inevitably argue.

A common labourer linking arms with a mechanical nun? There, both near the cathedral, strolling across cobbles under the dancing trees.

Gone, lost to the false city with its huddled buildings, and river pretending realness.

What manner of complex animals are us real ones? What have I become? Why should I have instilled – into the very nucleus – the equation x equals x, along with the nagging and burning desire to want to know what x is? Will I ever learn? Will the answer be my final thought?

That'll surely be synonymous with my first, whatever that was, belonging together as two sides of the equation. Neat bookends to the life, first and last, beginning and end, the question and the answer. Then the time miracle happens. I'll start again where I began. And the next question asked. Still more questions, questions. Waiter, bring me some brain brakes. Like a centrifuge, it's sending out innermost locked rooms to the edge. Doesn't anyone care?

16

'**D**on't you care? Do you always think of yourself? Bernadette, you're not speaking. You're becoming as bad as Dr Leibkov.'

'Because you haven't stopped yapping to let me get one word in.'

'What do you expect? Opening the wrong mindroom again, not in when I get home, no dinner ready. It's only fair. And you still haven't told me where you've been this afternoon.'

See that cunning smile mar her attractive face, glazed eyes leave mine and glance to the ceiling, cheeks flushing slightly.

'I'm stuck in the house all day – decided to go for a walk in the mall. Caught the bus.'

Already I'm becoming suspicious at this point, doctor, though I'll attempt to forge a barrier this time – a heavy steel shutter. I won't be exposed to any false truth.

'A long walk then. It's eight o' clock. I've been home for over an hour, waiting. I was that concerned, I was going to call the police.'

'The police? Whatever for?'

'I told you. I didn't know what happened. I've been pacing up and down. You won't wear your silver foil.'

Mock sympathy: 'Ah, poor thing. Just because the ropes tying me to the house came undone. Just because you let your slave escape.'

'I see what you're doing. One of your little tricks, this is.' At these words, she always seems to wonder what I'm insinuating, waiting for more fuel to feed the flames of the argument. Every time, every time, every time. Still I have to speak on. 'You're in the wrong. Then to cover your guilt, you turn the blame onto me.' Smug with my answer. 'Anyway, answer me this: there I am, looking out of the window...'

'And you wouldn't start a dinner for once.'

'Let me finish. Looking out, and all of a sudden you appear. Coming round the corner at the end of the road.'

'Haven't you got anything better to talk about? I've got the vegetables to put on.' I'll follow her into the kitchen.

'And I watch your progress towards the house.'

'Just shut up, Donald.' She has snatched down a saucepan from one of the wall hooks.

'Every step of the way — but there was no bus that passed along the main road. A bit odd, don't you reckon?'

She has stopped her movements, seeming to study the potatoes on the work surface. She's there for a century, turned to a pillar of salt until, quickly, her words shuffling into each other, she says, 'I went to Stuarts, got off the stop before. The bus would have passed before you started moping through the window. Any more questions for your enquiry, inspector, or can I make dinner?'

'What did you buy at Stuarts?'

'Clothes pegs. And before you ask they didn't have any.'

This will satisfy me. I've not much more to say to her for the rest of the evening. The dinner is absorbing; I can eat, and shuffle thoughts like a pack of cards at the same time.

Of course, everything she says is perfectly true. My wife wouldn't falsify. I didn't really see the car pull away from around the corner, and the driver turning to smile and wave. But the more I chew on the underdone vegetables, the more I can't stop thinking. I'll cut the visual snapshots into manageable pieces and chew on those.

But there he is again, turning and smiling and waving. And again, turning and smiling. And again, turning… I'll zoom onto his features in my mind's eye, like a cameraman, and when I see the smile – the bloody-toothed cat-smile – is showing below a black moustache, the anguish begins again like a vague headache. Sourceless, it's pervading, blunting my senses and dragging me down. Crash and burn. Though an explanation as to why Bernadette should be alighting from a stranger's car, and who that stranger might be, is easy to digest. This barrier has a fine set of holes to dilute the filmic frames.

As I see the person turning to wave for the fiftieth time – glimpse his striped jacket – it's already been sufficiently watered down to leave me with the decision that it didn't really happen. All I have here is a morbid fascination with a fiction.

Six feet of washed-out celluloid with the ends joined together, and it will loop and repeat, and be seen forever if wished. Though I don't wish. It's a small part only which wants this. The majority of me is getting queasy to the marrow.

But then I should have eaten my breakfast. And dinner yesterday. My guts are agitated. I need food. Give me sustenance.

17

Clacking of cutlery on plates and the murmuring of patrons, the occasional voice rising above the sounds as a porpoise might leap from the sea. Those fishing nets hanging from the ceiling have collected dust. And, as if smaller versions of themselves, spider's webs. Passers-by stop to inspect the menu tacked to the restaurant window. Some might come in and join the queue to the takeaway counter, where the proprietor serving will jut out his chin over the frying skate and cod to prompt the customer for his order. I've yet to hear this man speak. He communicates with flicks of fingers, movements of head and shoulder, a collection of mannerisms acquired over the years. For all I know, a deaf mute, reading lips before plunging the scoop into the trays or rattling the metal basket in the oil, or taking out a lump of fish from the glass cabinet.

Cheap prints adorn the walls. They have violent splashes of printing inks, no doubt covering cracks in the plaster and the worse patches of grease. I'll speak my order.

'Two egg and chips; two slices; tea?' the waitress rattles off.

Already she's back at my side, placing items on the scuffed melamine.

Let's cut away the white from the yolks to leave those disc pouches of runny yellow matter, willing to be impaled by a fried stick of potato. On the next table, a fat lady is putting a loaded fork to the mouth of her grimacing youngster. She's making the sound of a train. Wonderfully accurate impression.

A table of four women behind them is possibly another wind-up toy for each in turn leans forward to talk before sitting straight again to cut her food or eat. But they are doing this in a surprisingly consistent way, in rotation. Flies move in slow tangled zigzags above their scarved heads.

I find that if I concentrate on one group I'm able to isolate their conversation from the rest, and if I watch the flies or look to the scruffy floor, it becomes a consistent undertone again. Strangely though, the chug of a train behind this.

A shadow has fallen across my plate. You showing yourself at last, doctor?

'Tea,' speaks the bored waitress. She parks the cup and saucer before me, the brown liquid see-sawing to the lip. She's gone but her shadow persists.

'Would you mind if I share your table?'

I see this figure in silhouette, having his back to the bright window and a spotlight hiding within the netting drapes.

'Please do.'

He's sitting opposite me and I can view him more clearly. His head is as polished as a brown egg. As though someone has pulled hard down on his earlobes, his ears have settled too low with relation to his aquiline nose. Those eyes possess an indefinable strength and they seem to subtly change with the slightest of movement.

He has engaged my attention now, exposing his teeth. They are as white as a starched napkin and small and even, tending towards points more than the usual curves at their tips. So captivating is he that I'm left holding my fork with a limp chip impaled on the prongs.

He has paralysed me. I must break away from this binding spell. There, putting my arm down too quickly, I've knocked against the sauce bottle and it's rocking wildly and spinning slowly, somehow defying gravity as it moves towards the edge of the table. In an instant I've grabbed the bottle before it teeters over. Lumps of hard sticky brown have stained my hand.

This person is speaking with a fluidity unlike any other I have heard. The vocal quality is as appealing as an expensive, experienced perfume consisting of warm tones and subtle bass notes.

'One must be quick, otherwise you will be noticed. I am often noticed – I think it's because of my slight suntan.'

I'm normally reticent to speak with people I don't know yet this unique person has me formulating a reply. 'A good tan it is too.' He has a healthy shade washed into face and hands. But how curious indeed: he has no fingernails nor indentations where they should be. 'Have you been abroad?' I must add.

Ridges appear where eyebrows might once have been. The stranger begins a monologue in his low, rich voice.

'He sits alone in a room. There are many doors to this room. Each one will take him down corridors to similar rooms with yet more doors. There are no windows. The walls, floors and ceilings are of blue granite. In each of these rooms is a chair and a plain wooden table. Sometimes – though not often – he will discover other articles within a room, be it another piece of simple furniture or blocks of cut stone, or a jar of frogs. On one occasion, he found a clock hanging from a hook on the speckled wall. The second hand moves around to the twelve before turning back again, anti-clockwise, to the twelve; and thus it has continued. A lightbulb hangs from the ceiling in each room, held by a piece of green twisted flex. The lightbulbs never extinguish. There are no light switches. He has tried to unscrew the bulbs but they will not move; he has been unable to break them with the heel of his shoe, nor pull them from the ceiling by standing on a chair and hanging from the flex.

'There are no intervals, no sounds other than those he makes. Once, emerging from one of his rare sleeps, there was a noise, far away, like a distant trumpet, followed by a woman's laughter. He ran along many of the countless corridors and entered innumerable rooms although he never did find her that time. Sound has become the dropping of needles, metallic rain becoming ticking upon ticking becoming silent spaces filled with void. Such neat squares of loneliness.

'There she is, hidden in the folds of nothing...

'He knows nothing else but the doors and rooms and corridors. And the tables, chairs and lightbulbs, and the finds within rooms. He never grows older for he does not know what ageing is. He has spent many lifetimes studying the irregular texture of the walls, sometimes counting the grains he can see by pressing his nose to the surface.

'There was the time when he found a vase of flowers. Every bloom beautifully formed, each bottle-green stem tapering in a gentle curve, serriform leaves growing at regular intervals along each length. He wished to investigate these flowers, overcome any query in his study of them, comprehend them totally: to have observed and studied every part of every single flower; to have perceived the relationship of each petal with the next; to have compared and absorbed the subtle shading of each bloom with another; to be conversant in every sensory aspect, to the extent of being able to smell, taste and touch them in his mind – a mental depiction as total in all dimensions as the real items.

'However he was unable to finish this task. A sudden impulse made him step into a shadowless, evenly-lit corridor for a matter of seconds only. Upon his return, the flowers and vase had vanished. Despair is far from him, despite this; he doesn't grumble. It's only a matter of time before another discovery will stimulate his interest.

'Now he has found a room containing more than any other he has ever been into. He pours wine into a glass from a salmon pink stone pitcher. The liquid is stained by the yellow lamp light. He sips the wine. This is the first liquid he has ever tasted and it holds within it the miracle of life. There is a Christmas cracker lying beside a bread roll, and a butter knife, on a pine table. He picks up the cracker and takes an end in each hand before pulling outward. A difficult task and his face becomes red with the strain, and his mouth twists with the effort. It would require a minor adjustment: he perforates a line about the middle circumference with the knife. The cracker is more easily pulled into two parts, with a snap and the stench of sulphur. A crêpe paper hat – folded and tied with an elastic band – a scrap of paper, and a plastic whistle in the shape of a bird fall to the table, landing in a bowl of tomato soup before him. With a spoon he retrieves the three items from the soup. He lays the soggy scrap of paper and the folded hat and whistle upon the table beside the bowl. The elastic band is removed from the hat. Its vibrational quality is alpha two. He unfolds the hat and places it on his head. Taking the bird whistle by its hard beak he puts the fanned tail to his lips, and blows. It produces a sweet warbling and sputters tomato soup from the top of it. He inspects it and sees that the plastic moulding includes a worm in the beak of the bird, and that this worm is curled into the shape of the figure eight. If he were to break apart the whistle he would find inside another whistle, though much smaller, in the shape of a bird. If he would wish to break this one I should leave for him to decide, and what might be inside, let him discover. He might taste the soup and every so often his spoon would bring up another whistle from the red liquid, and he might notice the level of soup which never decreases, no matter how much he consumes. And if he were to look at the scrap of paper drying on the light wood of the table, he would find a simple amusement as one does from such pieces of paper from Christmas crackers. On one side it reads Please Turn Over and should he comply with this request, he will see the same words printed in neat blue letters on the reverse. You are a tortoise without its shell. Have a chip.'

He is pushing his plate towards me.

'No, really, thanks. A tortoise?'

'Vulnerable, sensitive, disturbed.'

'I don't think so. You've got me wrong there.'

As he turns away, my attention is released; I'm able to be aware of my surroundings until he is looking at me again, fixing me and capturing me once more.

'I think not,' he ventures. 'You are perhaps inhibited to divulge any problems. But consider, an unknown is the best sort to listen. Our lives have not crossed until now and after an unloading of your burden, I will take it away, and we shall never meet again.'

I'm strangely certain that what he says is correct. Quickly, for the smallest instant, I know who this man is but no sooner do I recognize him then I have forgotten.

Doctor, this isn't another of your disguises, is it? If so, you're swimming closer to the surface.

'I understand. I'll see myself reflected from you.

'It's my wife. She's a lovely person, believe me. And I do love her much, before you ask. I adore her. Our year of marriage has been good; very good. Lately though, we seem different together. We were like chemicals which combined in perfect chemistry, now we seem to react with each other. What has changed to allow this? I have headaches; it's as though she's acquired a shell. Inside is still the soft and gentle woman but this hard covering holds us apart. Can't seem to penetrate her.' I suddenly want to make light of my serious subject: 'In every sense.' I'm grinning to him but his neutral visage has extracted the puerile double entendre. 'Sex isn't everything, don't get me wrong. I could try to live without that, if only she'd be as she was, reachable and loving.

'I'm sure she loves me still. Though unable to show it lately.

'For the amount of time she spends in town, she never brings much shopping home. Perhaps she's meeting somebody but isn't that a ridiculous notion? Maybe there is something I've done yet I assume she's the one doing wrong.

'Money has become a bit worrying of late. We had to sell the car; I arranged for lifts into work. I'd become quite fond of the classic crate. Someone answered our advert and said he would come to view it the next day. Why can't it be a John, or a Peter, or a Simon here? I wish you'd help. I know the name I'm going to say, but can never seem to replace it.

'It was short notice to have the morning off so Bernadette said she would see him. You will know how twisted I'm becoming. When I arrived home that evening, my car was still outside and the potential buyer was in the living room. She had awaited his arrival for most of the day, she told me, and he confirmed this by saying he'd been there for only half an hour. It was the guy who reads cards and palms on the pier. It was Aaron. How to explain, both appeared agitated. He seemed more than uncomfortable but still loathe to leave. I hinted he should go, with or without the car. He bought it anyway.

I'll be honest I did feel a slight envy. He seemed alive, unencumbered with responsibilities I suppose, compared to me. His face wore a good-looking confidence.

'Bernadette seemed to hold an undertone of anger that evening. Several times she informed me of how annoyed she'd been at having to wait for the man to arrive. I tried to ask her questions like, what sort of coincidence was it that he, of all people, would buy our car? But she wouldn't answer.

'I make unsavoury ideas. I've tried to explain them. She's difficult to communicate with; I irritate her. I must expunge the uneasiness on my own; I have to erase these ridiculous feelings; reprimand myself for horrible considerations which are tainting my view of her. And why should they, when none of them are in accordance with fact? They're merely a product of my insecurities. Jealousy is a cancer and it must be arrested before it spreads.'

This unusual man has emanations from him. His ears have become transparent. I must wait for a reply but it seems as if his mouth has sealed. Indeed, if I lean closer, I can see the lips melded.

A finch has flown into the fish restaurant. It has landed on my table. Stabbing at a fried slug of potato, securing it in its beak and taking off again. Flying around the room before disappearing through the open doorway, the soggy chip twitching as though a jaundiced worm.

The startling man has gone. I didn't see him go.

The bird has returned with several other varieties. An owl has found a perch on the counter by the fryer. The proprietor is pushing his chin out as though expecting it to order. Nobody seems to be taking any notice: magpies flying from shoulder to shoulder, picking at bright earrings and necklaces with a clawed foot, or nudging the heavier shining cutlery with their beaks. A cockerel is crowing and hopping as though drunk, running for cover as a warthog comes trampling in, snuffling and squealing. Its small tusks catch on the table legs, taking wedges of wood from them. More animals – bleating sheep, dogs chasing them between the aisles, a host of monkeys swinging from the nets. A boisterous row.

This noisy animal army: these aren't animals. It must be a school outing. A cacophony of children, pushing and squabbling. Change your world quietly!

Doctor, can you see them?

I'm here. This is my station. Battle my way through the onslaught. I'm already three quarters of an hour late for work.

18

The train station was a vast area of brick, steel and glass. Pigeons flew high up in the vaulting and perched in rows on great metal spans, or roamed about the platforms pecking at invisible specks.

A dull pervading reverberation, broken only by a station announcement or trains moving out into the crisp daylight.

As Clement walked onto the concrete platform from the train, one of the schoolchildren, who had boarded earlier, gaped out from a carriage window. Those stone-hard eyes were neither interesting nor interested; a dispassionate stare only as though Clement was an exhibit at a museum. A man on the train turned away for a short time and his lips moved before another face joined him as a spectator. A woman at the far end opened the top of a window and was attempting to push her head through, while from a carriage door an arm held an accusing finger.

Embarrassment enveloped Clement though he felt a sense of satisfaction. The belief that he had become different in a mysterious way was being confirmed. If only Dr Leibkov was here in person, he told himself, he would see how correct I am.

But the satisfaction dissolved as some of his observers began to laugh openly. Clement's breath quickened. With humiliation joining his shame, he wanted to stop them, to turn their heads, and those heads seeming to rise and fall as if attached to weightless astronauts.

He turned abruptly away from his audience, brushed himself down and walked briskly to the ticket barrier. Once through, he went onto the station concourse.

His job would invariably involve much sitting and waiting. He visited the newsstand to buy a writing pad and a pencil before finding the exit and going into the city morning.

Like an insecticide sprayed bluebottle bouncing from ceiling to floor, so Clement had within him emotion which acted the same. He felt elation at starting work again but anxious at the possibility of finding his suitcases on the doorstep the coming evening.

Throngs of pedestrians brushed by, stern-faced and marching. The autumn morning had brightened even more but still it shone a cold light. A row of taxis sat in a line in sharp shadows, the drivers reading newspapers or sitting as if asleep. Pavement slabs beside them were still covered with frost, each like a spore under a microscope. Cars, buses and lorries buzzed past, vying for position along the road. The wide street was banked on each side with shops. There were offices above, high edifices towering into whiteness.

A senior citizen stood by an advertisement hoarding. Her eyes shone like beacons from their barren landscape. They fixed upon Clement as he passed.

'Would you like to know of eternal love?' she asked in a cracked voice. 'The day of judgement is upon us.' Her bare, sinewy arm described some esoteric symbol.

Clement wished to inquire if she was cold. Her skirt covered past her knees, a blouse over her frail frame. Her coat had been taken off, covering a pile of leaflets to prevent them from blowing away. She pushed a leaflet into Clement's hands.

Of course, she was as he, disciplined obsession shining. And see those illuminated organs: what did she perceive through them?

Then he nestled into the barely warm, living corpse and squinted out as if through oval windows.

There you are, Donald. But why is the neck into your shoulders, chin scraping your ribs? Of course, I see: sacks hanging like sandbags about your midriff, stuffed into pockets. And ectoplasmic ropes about each ankle, pulling more sacks which transform into misshapen forms without warning.

A car horn broke the spell. Just the stucco wall below the hoarding was before him, with a pile of leaflets fluttering at his feet and the old lady nowhere to be seen.

A disembodied station announcement reverberated from behind him as he walked away from the station.

Two women stood at the side of the main road waiting to

cross, their loose dresses from beneath their coats flapping like flags in the light wind. Duplicates, Clement immediately considered.

He took a turning along a side road. It was quieter there. He pulled up the collar of his overcoat and wished he had worn trousers instead of a skirt. He could change in an alley into clothes taken from his holdall but decided there was no time to spare.

The road funnelled the air into a biting wind. A sheet of newspaper came running up and frolicked about him before plastering itself over his legs. He tried to kick it off but it seemed glued to his tights. He stopped to remove the sheet of paper by hand and flung it away. The wind caught it again and it flew down the street like a kite.

This business with Mrs Froby, Clement muttered. It was her fault he didn't have the energy to walk fast. The impetus had left him, consumed with those chocolate bars an hour ago.

Dim reflections in shop windows, sometimes mimicking, down to the last foot flick, other times seeming in more of a hurry. At one point a reflection had ballooned out, his features distorting like a liquid plastic, all the while a ghost of a thing, with handbags and shoes showing behind.

He stopped. A fair reflection this one yet making him appear dowdy and advanced in years, his back bent with an invisible load.

A woman came out of a supermarket in a hurry as though being pursued and she threw hard glances behind, one of her arms lost in her shopping bag.

'Good morning, madam,' Clement felt he had to remark. She looked up with burning cheeks and a veil of concern before walking stiffly away. 'Very supreme, very typical,' he said.

A market sprawled untidily along another side road. The canvas canopies over the stalls billowed up and ropes wavered. A lady with the petite features of a field vole peeked attentively at a pile of carrots. Other women, clutching handbags or pulling shopping bags on wheels behind them, and men – appearing dazed as if hypnotized – wandered from stall to stall.

A lady turned to Clement, snickering. He was indignant but she looked past him to the stall opposite her. A cat stood on the produce, unaware of swipes from the stallholder's hand, just out of reach.

The animal moving now, fish-like.

Its body pulsed in an oscillatory fashion, waves moving along its spine then the length of its tail; and before the next pulse, the tip of the tail pointing, like a finger would, to a pile of oranges. Clement was excited at the spectacle.

'That cat's something I can't explain,' he said out loud.

How to invigorate the next plane of understanding so as to comprehend this extraordinary act. He turned away to register reactions of others, no doubt struck with awe. But no – the stallholder whose stall had been chosen for this rite had ignored the cat to serve another customer.

A clatter of thoughts came to Clement in a surge.

Don't you understand what you're missing? Before you, ancient symbolism described yet you're not interested. We should commune, come together in ceremony. A small slice of wisdom here, another there, for the encompassing map once more to be seen. Will this archaic enlightenment be allowed to decay, each part wither with each owner? Will nobody see with me and try to dissect these rituals? That cat shows us a piece of the whole. As does the hot chestnut man holding his mittened hands over the brazier; and that signpost, and the guy standing by it spitting into the gutter. A masterful act performed with silent wit. Surely suggesting a cornerstone of the esoteric.

While Clement mused, he weaved his way through the market aisles, his attention caught by an apron or a gesture, or a rotting tomato smearing the walkway, and each time he felt he might glean some meaning.

He bought two apples before moving on. He knew it had been an important act to buy them. Quite why, he was unsure. For certain though, it was yet more significance, more synchronicity.

By buying the apples a positive wave has been created. Do I ask for thanks or payment of any kind? No, this is how transparent I've become.

Yet why do I still fumble in the branches of the darkest mindrooms like an ape unable to evolve? It has to be the infesting filmics. Some fierce, taken on a mountainous form, too big to cope with. No wonder my barriers need to be large, though many have been destroyed already. I'm surprised parts of me haven't begun to dissolve. Or maybe they have, though being such a creeping process I'm unaware of it.

Soon I'll discover the force which binds us, stopping us from flying apart. But then what if I fail? Tyres would become rubber sap and run into gratings; cars collapsing as their metals resolve into slews of molten steel. Timber breaking down to cells. Bricks becoming sludge. Skin evaporating to leave pads of muscle, ropes of sinew. Bones crumbling to chalk, a soup of chemicals, liquids and gases. A return to the primordial broth.

My ears can capture you again at last, doctor. Of course this is impossible, I'll grant you.

Though you never believe a word I say, whether truth or lies. Who are you to sift over my mind's contents like someone at a jumble sale, accepting some but rejecting others? You haven't the ability to discriminate. I would guess if you were to extract a slice of fiction along with a slice of fact, you would find they have very similar forms. Doctor, you surely wouldn't be able to find any difference because I can't and I own these thoughts.

I mean, had she really spoken to me like that or was it a nasty drama constructed in weary confusion?

Get up, lazy slob, I think she said.

I'm struggling to open glued eyes; my body had found a position so sublime and comfortable; I've melted into the bedclothes with a delicious warmth. This fight to a higher state is like wading through treacle.

Her words are slowly being understood.

'Wake up, idiot.'

19

Am I hearing correctly? Perhaps I've inadvertently dragged dream state into waking life. 'What did you say?'

My tongue feels swollen to twice its size and layered with a bitter fungus.

She sits in front of the dressing table at a side of the bedroom. Holding a lipstick to her lips, the reflection copying. Perhaps it was only for mirror life her words were meant. She's showing surprise. 'You're awake. I said nothing.'

'What time is it?'

'Time you got up.' Her expected reply. My muscles have been injected with powdered stone. 'Shift yourself. You know if I leave before you get moving, you'll be there for half the day.'

A concentrated effort – I'll move to a sitting position. Bernadette is thickening her eyelashes with mascara.

'Putting on a lot of makeup. Never used to put that much on.' A front door slamming from somewhere down the street and the background chatter of birds. 'I don't like you with so much. Would you wipe it off for me? One of your best dresses you've put on, isn't it? Why do you have to work on a Saturday anyway? What if…'

'Just belt up for a change.'

'Nice. Just trying to make conversation.'

She's standing to adjust her dress. 'That wasn't conversation, that was a lecture.'

I'll give a chuckle in the hope of lessening the serious mood we're falling into.

'I'm a bit jealous; the slinky dress you're wearing. Those men at the office staring. Surely you must like me being jealous?'

She's gone to the wardrobe and retrieved her coat. A man in a white tunic is walking past her, holding a ladder.

'Listen, I don't want to argue. You dare make me late. I'd lose my job. But then you'd like that.'

She's putting on the coat. Someone is loading up a barrow with produce from a store next to a market stall. Drone of traffic from the end of the road.

I've picked up a watch from the bedside cabinet. 'Yes I would, as it happens. It was underhand the way … hang on, it's only seven. You've got at least another hour.'

It's her turn to laugh but the chimes have become a discordant jangle. 'Starting earlier than I thought.'

'Well, at least give me a kiss.'

She tuts as though an effort for her. Walking over to the bedside, bending, pecking me on the cheek like an aunt might an invalid nephew.

I'll grab her wrists and pull her down on top of me. I have my mouth pressed to hers but my tongue is licking her lipstick. I run my hand down the line of buttons and despite her struggling, and shouts of the robot stockholders, can deftly unbutton the coat in a swift motion. This excited burning within is pressing me on. My hand is massaging one of her breasts. I've rolled her over and my other hand has found her suspender belt. I've paused at this. I always pause. The blunted electric jolt, the question: why should she wear such exotic lingerie to work? The more defined jolt below my waist, passion demanding I continue, a sweet savagery taking me over.

She's managed to wriggle out from under me, panting heavily and looking furious. Her tangled hair needs combing and one of the coat buttons is hanging from a thread. The screech: 'You swine!' The astonishing announcement: 'How dare you. How dare you touch me.'

Shocked, discharged from an unreal place. The words echoing back and forth like a hurtful tennis volley. I can never catch them, unable to replace them. 'What do you mean? I'm your husband. Can't I even kiss you?'

She's rebuttoning her coat. Traffic from the main road louder still, imaginary but constant. Stream of pseudonyms flowing by, walking the cardboard pavements, more within their grumbling vehicles jostling on the highway.

She rummages in her handbag for her compact mirror.

Retrieving it, she'll open it to inspect her face and wipe smears of lipstick from about her mouth with a tissue. Any second.

There. This girl here is not my wife. My wife was a gentle, loving person. Someone has stolen her and is inhabiting her body.

'Leave me alone. Don't you dare lay one finger on me again without asking permission.'

'You must be joking.' I'll hold my hand up to her. 'Let me caress you. Take the elastic band of recuperations.'

'It's my body. You've no right to touch me. I'll decide who can and who can't.' She's walking out of the bedroom onto the landing. Her footsteps are heavy on the stairs. She's wearing her high heels, clopping across the lino in the hall. The door squeaking open. And the slamming of it comes at precisely the same time as the hooting of a car's horn.

Merrily, merrily, merrily, merrily...

I must rid myself of this solid clump of despair beginning to live within. Curling in my chest, sending out filaments, it's found its way through spaghetti tangles of intestines. Infected my lungs and is surely squeezing my heart so tightly it's bringing tears to my eyes.

Bring her back, let the front door be the door of the cocoon. The wardrobe exit will be her entrance back to me. A shifting, change in appearance, a seething mass of intricate bands soothing with fragile tones, creating chords of deepest love which fade to infinity. Still, don't touch me emanates from her throat, out from her maroon lips; clopping on lino becoming the chopping of adoration, a mutilating, mutating into worse than chopped liver; the front door slam, a thump in the foundations of my deepest barriers, splinters slashing, till she emerges again from the wardrobe, pouting as though ready to kiss except don't touch me becoming scraping shards of smouldering coal, scorching the bands of tenderness...

This mindroom is mere fiction.

I daren't look at the companion watches tightening about my wrist. The cold metal is melting into the flesh. Not my fault the train was delayed; this they must understand.

Many replacements here today. They can't all be late, except perhaps for that automated creature running past like a frightened bird.

Increase my pace, eat up yards of road. I'm not far off.

How many steps could I count before becoming number blind? Hammerings within my breast, the many breaths I've taken, millions of words spoken.

Who's there to remember me when I've ceased to be? Mrs Froby for one. She thinks I owe her the rent.

Move the feet, drag miserable diluted shadow behind. See it run into other shadows cast by the shops like puddles of rain would. What sort of residue do these shadows leave? What imperceptible remnant?

I don't give a damn if you think my theories far-fetched. I suspect, in truth, you're jealous.

'Not so.'

Welcome again. But still a quick and flippant reply. You're giving one of those funny smirks.

'Donald, you don't need theories. Unclutter, rid yourself of them.'

How I'm being buried by your impossible directions.

Look at that woman wearing the bizarre spotted hat. Can you imagine her not whining like a dog over what life means? Or the man jauntily swinging the duck-head walking stick. Does he appear upset in the least, living with his barriers?

An aeroplane droning overhead. Can you hear it?

I wouldn't get too comfortable snuggling here, offering your sickly sugar-hiccup advice. I wouldn't turn your back on me either, otherwise, with an almighty push, you'd be out. I suppose whatever part of you is infiltrating might be ejected in wavering streams. Then it'll be my turn to nod with sympathetic understanding while you're trampled and kicked about by pedestrians.

Or I might choose to be rid of you in one long drawn-out gas stream to peacefully disperse, your condescension becoming the merest whisper.

My threats have no effect. Are you indestructible, like a barrier?

'I am your liberator. Guard me well.'

Hearing you, doctor, but still can't see you. Show yourself. Enough skulking behind my frontal lobes. How many others have another, mounted over their forehead like a jockey on his horse? Why have you chosen me?

'You have chosen yourself. Face the truth. Expunge your distress.'

Easy for you to say. Looking at you shrugging, I expect your boulder head to topple off. I've such unexpected powers: with one prod of my metaphysical wand, and there, flames leap crimson from your neck. A brace of squirming snakes, Medusa-like. This is to represent your poisonous ideas.

But you can too easily supersede my abilities. Already remoulding your head. A strong chin, that one. Thick bush of a moustache on your upper lip. Doctor, you don't have a moustache. Those dark eyes, swarthy skin. Take off the striped jacket, I prefer the tweed. You're trying to disturb me on purpose, and this wouldn't be the first time.

I can dredge up another filmic in a sealed mindroom, a shocking incident, is that what you want? I'm starting to think you've got a perversion, a kinky desire to listen to me stammering my way through embarrassing experiences, with the lame excuse it's necessary to unpack the mindrooms. Won't you allow me at least one barrier?

Memories of my love-life are smutty piles of refuse. Echoes of them mock me. Halfway through the act of lovemaking I begin to cry for I know I'm losing her. She's become an empty shell; then for her to start laughing before pushing me away? Why should you have made me remember that? If only feeling and commitment had been present, then it would have been relevant. And I wouldn't have been reduced to a slobbering goblin.

I need to erect barriers as massive walls, but still the hurt builds a lead block. And with terror of being smothered alive, it places the dense slab over me, plunging me into a dank, black box of self-contempt and despair.

All I can tell you is, if I'd been given a sharp knife then, I would have gladly sliced off my private parts with one cut. And as the blood leaps out I'd run to her and bellow with a potency found from high martyrdom: see what you've made me do, I've de-sexed myself for you! No longer will I be encumbered with its tensions and demands. We can live a meaningful life without sex, and so without pain, a spiritual bonding other men will envy.

My barriers I wish to keep but the lead slab pressing on me I'd gladly give to you, doctor.

This tall concrete block: you're reflected in all of those windows. 'No barriers,' you call out with multiple voices.

You've obviously never understood a single syllable I've spoken.

Let me tell you this much. If my barriers do completely decay, then you must know I hold you responsible for the consequences.

20

The windows of the office block reflected only a sombre premonition of the day. Each square of glass was a drab vacuum. As he looked upward, Clement had a dizzying sensation as the massive structure seemed to lean forward. A sign on the building named it as Falcon House. Clement entered via the revolving door into a foyer and called, 'Klipper? Klipper?' Without a response, he made the decision to become Donald again; this was no work for Donadette. He found the lavatory to change before coming out of the building in search of the security guard.

Over the gusting wind, a man roared from across the street, 'Mr Clearmint, that you?' Clement turned quickly to see him leaving a café and as the fellow hurried over the road, he shouted again, 'That you?'

He was small though overweight and from his abundant body protruded a worm of a neck. This neck supported a bony, thin-skinned head with stark features upon it. Charcoal eyes seemed embedded deeply within their sockets, his forehead hanging heavily under a peaked cap. There were two pens in the top pocket of his blue uniform. He scowled and poked Clement in the chest.

'Where'd you get to? Been waitin' half an hour.' He wiped an arm across his mouth before adjusting his cap.

'Dreadfully sorry but trains and Donadette and the doctor, you see.'

The man put his hands upon his heavy hips. 'Should be telephonin' agency, understand? Get inside.'

The foyer was warm. A tropical plant stood as high as the lift doors. On one side of the lift was a flight of stairs which rose up the building as its spiral backbone. A second flight on the other side disappeared into the basement. In the left corner was a curve of padded seats. The building style with its outdated interior design had not changed in fifty years.

They sat. Clement saw the glass-fronted reception area and was about to ask a question when he was cut short.

'Well, Mr Clearmint. Like the look of you and that ain't often. Bein' security makes you treat everyone with suspicion. Guilty till proven innocent; least, my motto. Soon get a habit of scrutinizin'. Believe me, might be the difference between another cuppa and a knife between the ribs.'

'How long have you existed in this job? Klipper, is that your agency label? Agency. Sounds like spying, government, those kind.'

He was puffing out his cheeks. 'Just because I like you, don't mean you can take advantages. Only mates who know me for ages call me Klipper.'

'Didn't mean to offend.'

'Alright then,' was Mr Klipps' reply and he rubbed his paunch. 'Could tell agency about lateness, but tell you what.' He threw his sight to the left and right. 'Favour deserves another, get my meanin'?' Clement nodded. 'Meant to show you the ropes. How to open up, shut up, set alarms. No cleaners again for three months till new company starts. Two months after, start renivatin'. Got to learn about boiler. Agency says not necessary but I'm old school. Keep record of visitors. Take a few hours; agreed?' Clement was unable to tear his sight from the carpet tiles. He began to count them. 'Come right out, Mr Clearmint. Need to leave early, before twelve. Won't be here tomorrow either. Can't tell you why.' Mr Klipps moved nearer and Clement smelled coffee and stale tobacco. 'So don't tell 'em about me leavin' off early; won't tell 'em about you being late. Been eating sweets? Got a red mouth.' He sat back in the seat as though surprised by his own words.

The security guard got to his feet with a grunt and trotted over to the reception office on his stumpy legs. His fingers ran along the sill below the window there before opening the office door. He went in. Clement saw him through the pane of glass looking like a bloated fish in its tank then heard his muffled voice saying, 'Quick, had a late start.'

Clement joined him. As Mr Klipps carefully brought down a uniform hanging from behind the door, Clement leaned on the counter and inspected the foyer through the office window. It seemed much larger that way. The revolving door was there to his left and he saw pedestrians walking by along the cold street.

Mr Klipps cleared his throat and prodded Clement in the back. 'Enough daydreamin', change in gents. Be snappy.'

21

The white tiles on the floor, the whites of the walls and urinals, and the sinks like a row of a skull's teeth, seemed to reflect coldness. Light from the fluorescent strips spread a chill bath about the room. The doors to the water closets formed a wall to one side.

Clement took off his overcoat and hung it on a hook next to a long mirror. He avoided catching his reflection; shuddering breath as he untied the laces of his shoes and took the shoes off. The stone floor tiles sent cords of ice through the soles of his feet.

He changed into the uniform. The padding of the jacket was a comforting grip on his shoulders.

Only dripping water from a cistern. But after, rustling – he froze.

The sterile atmosphere within the colourless room was affecting him, making him agitated and nervous. He urinated in a urinal, throwing glances over his shoulder to the row of doors. Then with a hand still tugging at his zip, and staring about suspiciously, he went over to retrieve his overcoat and trousers, both crumpled by a washbasin. He was not going to be caught off guard. He called out in a worried tone, 'Who is it?'

An abrupt cough as though someone was trying to clear his throat, coming from behind one of the closet doors. Clement held his breath before marching over and rapping upon the doorframe. 'Who's in there?' he demanded indignantly. 'Come out and show yourself. You have no right to be in this building.' His voice had found an unusual firmness. He put his ear closer to the door. The rustling of leaves again. He instantly recognized it as a drawn-out sigh. 'If you don't come out, I'll be forced to take action.'

'I can't come out,' was the quick retort. Although said as if in a hurry, each word had been weighed down with sorrow.

'Why ever not?'

The dripping cistern again for a full minute. Clement gathered up this time and condensed it to a mere snap of the fingers for mutual benefit. Already he knew the identity of the person behind the toilet door. This man constructed his replies as carefully as an architect plans a municipal building, his use of sovereign silence as forceful and inspirational as elements an artist judges to leave out.

'My form will not allow me to be seen. I've become as nothing on earth.'

Clement was taken aback. 'What's happened, Dr Leibkov? Who could have done this?'

'You!' roared the doctor and this one word spiralled like a whirlpool.

'But how? I didn't wish you any harm. I wanted you to leave certain mindrooms and leave barriers alone.'

A rattling exhalation came from within the closet with such a forlorn sweep it sent shudders of despondency through Clement. All manner of surreal pictures visited him, possible forms of what Dr Leibkov might have become. He allowed the doctor to punctuate the silence with sighs and coughs until Clement asked, 'Can you ever be as you were?'

'If you will allow it. I suspect this: should I dare to gaze upon myself, I would be appalled into a stupor. And should you ever see me, you would be transmogrified. You would become no less than what I have become. If I'm able to look at you, however, then once more will I become human.'

Clement creased his forehead. 'You're saying, if you look at me, we'll be the same but to look at you I'll become a horrible monstrous creation.'

'This is the paradox we must tackle,' wheezed the doctor, his voice grown thin and sibilant.

'You sound different. You must be ill.'

'I am constantly changing from one demented form into another, a slow, insidious mockery of the flesh. At any time, I might not have the ability to see but only have to wait a brief while before I have many eyes, rooted into an erupting corpulence which I have become.' He spoke in a rumbling thunder. 'We must never be together again. I have persistent apprehension, I'm unable to shift it: you will transform as I have, no longer—' A horrendous shriek cut the doctor's sentence short.

'How can I let you suffer? Let me in. You have a chance to become like me.'

A modulated trilling. 'Only if you give up your barriers and unlock the rooms behind them. This is the advantage for us.'

'You know I can't.'

'It's for that very reason I've been modified beyond recognition. I left you on my own accord, this is true. But for me to have stayed any longer would have held you back. You're progressing well, Donald. You may still visit whenever you feel the need. I'm always available. I have given you my home number. Take a firm hold of your own life. You have the power; banish those remaining barriers. We know, don't we, they are unnecessary. Cast them aside, give them up, donate them to me.'

Clement was infuriated and he stabbed a reply. 'Your superior intellect hasn't helped you this time, doctor. I'm wise to your game. Like a thief in the night you stalk me and should I throw down my guard for a second, you'll snatch away my armour. Come out; why don't you face me in true combat!'

But as he knocked upon the doorframe once more, he noticed a curve of metal with "vacant" inscribed on the lock. 'Ha,' Clement yelled, 'it's open!'

Distant and imploring, 'I beg you, don't come in.'

22

The hinges let out a slow creak as the door was pushed. Clement put one arm up as a shield with the other arm clutching his belongings.

The closet was empty.

He stared to the bowl of the lavatory pan. The water was an unnatural blue from the disinfectant block within it. He pulled the chain and watched the spinning water without emotion of any kind.

As if coming out of a trance he rubbed his face with a leg of the old trousers before hurrying back to the foyer.

'Took your time. Made a cuppa,' Mr Klipps said.

Clement sat on a wooden chair which was pushed to the back wall of the reception office. He gratefully sipped the hot beverage from a mug. Mr Klipps picked up a thick blue volume, brushing grains of sugar from it.

'Visitin' book,' he announced. 'Visitors got to sign.' He noticed Clement looking intently to the counter. Mystified, he looked there also and quickly comprehended. Clement had not been given his uniform cap. Mr Klipps handed it over, saying, 'What you're after? Right too. Must respect uniforms.' Clement put on the hat. 'Been in army? No, 'spect not. Did my bit.' Mr Klipps paused to drink. His epiglottis rose and fell in his scrawny neck. He sat opposite Clement, who was contemplating the light fitting stuck in the middle of the ceiling looking like a single, huge barnacle. 'Candles once,' Mr Klipps commented, the memory inspired by Clement's interest above him. 'Power cut, see. Accountancy firm upstairs in those days, sat about chattin'.'

Clement allowed another silence to come between them. He was enjoying the tea. He adjusted the cap. Already his scalp itched with the warmth created beneath it. A clock above the window whirred then fell silent again.

A peculiar thought came to him. The fat security guard must have had a head transplant. That would account for the discrepancy between the slim skull with the thinnest of skin layers upon it and the short and overweight torso to which it was apparently attached. Had this man decided to abandon his soul within his original thinner frame? What type of soul had he offloaded – a water soul, fire or stone soul, a soul pilloried by laboured memories of the abandoned life? And what of the soul he was in charge of? Does he wrangle with the differences? It didn't seem right. He was about to mention an aspect of it when Mr Klipps spoke before him.

'Quiet one you are, Mr Clearmint,' he said with a chuckle.

'S'pose why you got the job. Agency likes quiet ones. Meant to get on 'stead of yappin'.' He tried to put his elbows up and back onto the counter top but succeeded only in jogging the telephone. 'Still, too many words left unsaid sometimes then bang — too late.'

'Saving words,' Clement began. 'Fine specimens worthy of capture. Here's some: define refine. You see? Now refine define. Then…'

'Perhaps you're right,' interrupted Mr Klipps. He took another gulp of tea and continued, 'Person can talk too much. Two extremes, happy balance what's wanted.' The clock whirred again but this time was followed by ten electronic pips. He drew in a sharp breath. 'Time's pushin'. Finished tea, haven't we. Must start. Follow me.'

He led Clement out to the side of the reception office where a cupboard stood beside the lavatories. He unlocked it and fumbled around the back of the doorframe for a light switch. A small bulb illuminated a control panel tucked inside. There were rows of green, red and yellow lights, and dials and switches upon its fascia. It appeared to be complicated. Clement glared at the appliance with suspicion.

'Very simple,' Mr Klipps was saying. 'Clever tricks here for alarms, heatin', lightin'. Eight o'clock, followin' procedures.'

He began to relate the pertinent aspects of the system, sometimes turning one of the switches or pressing buttons; and occasionally looking to Clement to ensure his instructions were being understood. Clement was nodding and grunting affirmations, even though the explanation given didn't seem to be making much sense. The harder he tried to concentrate on the man's words, the more jumbled and comical they were sounding. Didn't Mr Klipps understand just how preposterous his talking was? Possibly the nonsensical syllables were meant as a joke. He did let out a snigger but disguised it by sniffing.

Without warning the novelty of the situation vanished and meaning was there again.

'Clear? Questions?' asked Mr Klipps.

'As clear as a daydream. But why the flashing and glittering?'

The security guard appeared puzzled. His eyelids slowly closed before springing open. 'Variation in light – what you mean – in bulbs?' He put a hand to his chin, rubbing it thoughtfully while studying Clement.

Clement became as confused as the guard leaning against the cupboard door. When spoken, the sentence had seemed appropriate and full of meaning but now he was not sure what he had meant.

Mr Klipps' face cleared a little. 'Nothin' to worry about. Variation in electric current. Twinkle a bit. Perfectly normal. Anyhow, boiler room next.'

23

They took the steps beside the lift with care, the lighting leading down to the basement barely adequate. Once in the cramped gully of the concrete flight, Clement was confronted with three doors. He was informed that the two doors either side were more cupboards as he followed the waddling man through the third.

The basement was cool, and smelled of oil and dampness. By the mustard light from the bare bulbs hanging from the ceiling the concrete floor was seen to be stained with brown patches. The lifeless walls − stretches of unplastered blockwork − seemed to take a step nearer as Clement tried to study them from the periphery of his vision.

A partition divided the basement into two areas. Within the unlit section were filing cabinets and degenerate computers moping in the shadow, and typewriters dumped on the floor. In the half-light they looked like an undiscovered species of beetle, massive but calcified.

A network of ducts ran along the walls and grew out from

the floor and ceiling of the main section. It was as if at one time the pipes had large polished leaves hanging; might have been the plump stems of a metallic vine.

Some of the pipes found their way to the huge copper boiler dominating the basement. Mr Klipps had tottered up to the device and was tapping the glass of one of the pressure dials. 'System's dead,' he stated. 'Central on every two weeks, keeps mould away. Cold up there, use electrical heater under the counter.'

After being told the redundant boiler still needed to be maintained in case of an emergency, Clement asked if he could go outside. He had come over feeling faint.

'S'pose you'd better.' Clement turned to leave but Mr Klipps took him by the arm. 'Don't make a habit of this, do you?'

Clement moaned weakly, 'Boiler room; demanding; heavy.'

'Bit costaphrobic, if you ask me. Off you go then. Good job you don't have to stoke Bessy.' He waved over the front of the formidable boiler. It held authority and Mr Klipps paused as though to acknowledge its presence with respect before saying, 'Wouldn't make a routine of nippin' out. Agency check up every month.' Clement tried to gulp air to lungs seeming to have become shrivelled. 'Not at your post, sacked. Simple as that. Have to go out once awhile though. Expected, but always lock up.' Clement was licking his dried lips as a mauve filter was put before him. The intensity of light halved. As though the guard had crawled inside the boiler, his words were dulled and echoed as if by the thick layers of copper. 'Least ways, I expect it. Agency don't, tell you that much for nothin'. War starts, at your desk. You alright? Better go before you drop.'

The quick air in the street rejuvenated Clement. He marched back into the foyer. He rubbed his palms together and shuddered for it was still a wintry morning. Mr Klipps was coming out of the reception office.

'Told you hours?' he enquired. 'Good.' He glanced at his watch. 'Right, me done; time I was off. Should have shown offices, but you can do it yourself, can't you? Instructions written about what I've said. Have a rummage, you'll find 'em. Here's the keys. Key map somewhere in reception. Anyway, Mr Clearmint.' He enthusiastically pumped Clement's arm with an energetic handshake and wished him well. Then, just before he was swallowed up by the revolving doors, he called back, 'Remember, one good turn.'

Clement saw him spat out onto the street. He scuttled away on his stubby legs at an admirable speed.

After washing the mugs and tidying up, Clement looked in the drawers and cupboards under the counter. There were a few items of interest but still not enough to capture his attention. He sat and eventually closed his eyes.

Apart from deadened sounds of traffic and the anonymous ticks of the office clock, there was silence.

The confines of the office had become his enclave, a private domain which nobody could encroach upon. The movements of the city belonged to another dimension, an alien and hostile environment. His was the only true, safe place despite hunger and thirst gnawing at his constitution.

He tried to empty his mind, to become physical self only. The task was a difficult one. No sooner had he got rid of the last scrap, another thought would come bustling in.

'You there.' He decided to make a final concerted effort. 'Are you deaf?'

He fought to regain sense of surroundings and there, quickly, in sharp focus, someone stood looking through the pane of the reception office window. Clement went to meet him in the foyer.

'Wondered if you might be asleep,' said the man without humour.

'Sleeping the sleep of sequence,' Clement answered.

'I'm trying to locate St Margaret's Crescent. I've an appointment there very soon and do you think I can find it? Been round the block three times already.'

Clement's stomach spoke with a gurgling, sounding like water draining from a sink. He went back into the office and pulled open a drawer to produce a map. He brought it back out and unfolded it carefully, laying it onto the carpet tiles of the foyer. Both men crouched down, resting on their haunches, to inspect the city's intricate nervous system displayed in lines of red, black and blue.

The visitor jabbed a finger onto the map. 'Here we are. This is us here, right? So…' He placed both palms flat down and leant forward as if about to perform a handstand. It seemed to Clement as though he had solidified there, on the foyer carpet, becoming a piece of sculpture for other visitors to admire. But no sooner had he thought this, the man pushed himself up to stand. 'Around the corner, next right, next left; thanks.' He went out quickly. The movement of the revolving door displaced a wedge of coldness into the foyer. Clement shuddered but remained crouching for a while, following the meandering course of a road on the map until it ran out to the west.

When he returned to the reception office he remembered the apples bought in the market. He retrieved one of the green fruit from the paper bag in his holdall and bit: it tasted of soap. Disappointment but he felt grateful, for at least the spell had been broken which had overtaken and anaesthetized him.

A pack of playing cards lay on a small table. Clement emptied the box of its contents and shuffled them before laying two face down, then putting the palm of his hand over one of them. If he relaxed and focused attention he was sure the front image of the card would declare itself.

The telephone rang. He blinked and stiffened. The ringing was rude and clamorous in his quiet capsule. He was indignant for the intrusion into his privacy. No need to answer, it would stop soon enough.

Like a solid which can become liquid then gas, all can transmute to sound, if not from without then originating from within, he concluded.

Perhaps he was the generator. Sonorities, trembling resonances, setting up oscillations to reach a climax of unbearable plangency, bells clanging with a furor and with surging tones of such unparalleled power as to become firm again…

To solidify into a telephone, ringing insistently, never letting up until Clement leaned over and lifted the receiver to his ear.

24

'**S**even of hearts,' a female voice said quietly from the other end of the line. Clement brought the telephone to the table and turned over the playing card.

'How did you know that?' he asked with surprise. 'How'd you possibly know? Unless, I suspect, you were born with the gift, a rare talent bestowed to the few. You're able to take the phenomenon of cause and effect and reverse it, am I right? Would you teach me this? I've a serious use for such a discipline. But then, perhaps it's trickery after all. Like your palm-reading friend. He's not to be believed.'

'Not so. Quite a few things he told me have come true.'

'Like what? Tell me just one if you can.'

'You wouldn't be interested.'

'Of course I would. Wouldn't have asked otherwise.'

There was a pause from the other end before she said, 'My job.'

Clement gripped the telephone receiver harder: any aspect concerning Bernadette's new job angered him. He sucked in his bottom lip and tried not to speak but words flowed under their own pressure. 'I see; yes, I understand. He told you about the job; told you how you were going to deceive your husband.'

'I didn't—'

'And that you were going to…' he searched for the right expression, 'harm our marriage.'

An interruption of laughter and so loud, Clement had to pull the receiver away from his ear.

'Harm our marriage!' she echoed. 'I'll tell you Donald, if our marriage has been harmed as you call it, it happened well before I got the job.'

'What are you saying? What do you mean?'

'Listen, I'm not prepared to argue anymore. I've got my job and that's that. There's no more to be discussed.'

'OK,' he said finally, 'you can have your job and I won't take it away.'

She laughed again but this time in mockery. 'Won't, you say? Can't, more like.'

Clement spoke with a tremble. 'Alright, can't. But shouldn't we be friends again? I do love you deeply, Binny. I sometimes think if there's like on one side of love, there might be hatred on the other. No intermediate state. You don't fall out of love and land up feeling neutral. Understanding me? Want us to love and like, before it's too late. Don't want us to leave love behind in our silly squabbles. Not that I could ever hate. Never could.' There was silence at the other end of the telephone.

'Never hate, always love you,' he said loudly, the words catching in his throat.

'Who is this?' another voice demanded and the quality of it sounded different.

'We're pulling ourselves apart. Let us reunite.'

'I'm sorry, I think I've got a wrong number.' There was a click before the telephone line became a lifeless hum.

With annoyance, Clement dropped the receiver back onto its base.

Again, solemn introspection. He slumped in the chair and stared blindly into space. When the clock above the window whirred, he threw a hateful glance for being disturbed, and the machine was silenced. The blunt ticking became quieter, each fine tick, no larger than a grain of salt, falling and collecting as fragile transparent stalactites, hanging down from the counter to the vinyl-tiled floor.

He wanted to vandalize the delicate structures though he knew, with the insistent progression of time, it would not take long before they were built again.

The activity was beginning to annoy him. He did think to find a vacuum cleaner to suck the whole lot up but remembering the pencil and pad he had purchased; the thought was forgotten. He felt an urge to write, to clarify important topics.

He got the items from his overcoat pocket and pulled the chair closer to the table by the back wall.

No sooner had he held the pencil in readiness, ideas fled.

All that remained was potential, a compulsion to express himself only. The white rectangle of the pad with its feint blue lines mocked him. He nervously went to chew the pencil the wrong end. He tasted bitter graphite.

He dare not disgrace the dignity of the fresh page with any randomness. What is to be expressed must be essentially fundamental, he told himself. Perhaps he should write on a scrap of paper, to prepare and modify the script until perfection is achieved. Only then would it be fit for the pad, written with care in his best handwriting.

He had been scribbling jagged lines on the corner of the first page. He was despondent then; the purity had been desecrated, its virginity taken without ceremony. Should he rip this page from the spiral binding? He decided not to; he would use it to work out a piece of prose before committing it – exactly and succinctly formulated – to a fresh clean page.

A stream of inconsequential words flowed through his brain, the one insisting the formulation of a cousin: 'Coin, cone, clown, crown, brown, bain, drain, train; rain, sane, seen, sown, sawn, lawn, pawn…'

He tapped the side of his tipped head as if the words would empty out from his ear. Then he plunged in, and wrote:

Dissolving of Veal the Tanner was gradual, gradual. Started on autumn night when skies were bruised – hard tracery of dead branches clawed against the real moon. Walking to cottage, in the past valley, twisted hunchback disturbing him by whistling tuneless dirge. Reminiscent of a sailor who, many years long since departed, did whistle up a storm.

What is that tune?

Question best left unanswered. Turn of the heels hunchback crawls into orchard, apples shrivelled in the slugged grass.

Veal arriving home. Wife looks up from knitting. Perished rubber at marked changing of husband's appearance.

Hunchback lope between mossy trunks. Rabbit scream while torn by owl talons.

Hesitant wife standing. Gently places hand upon Veal's hand. Two hands. Veal the Tanner becoming so scarecrow scarecrow, expected rustle of straw.

Clement leaned back in the wooden chair to view the story. He read through the piece twice and crossed out a few of the adjectives. He was pleased with the result. He turned the page, being ready to write it again in a neater hand, but was dismayed to find he had been using too much pressure: there was his story in stencil. Maybe he shouldn't worry; use the notebook for initial workings and purchase a new notebook to write it again precisely and neatly. He might buy a fountain pen and a bottle of blue-black ink to do the job properly.

He was feeling peculiar. Like the way Mr Klipps' instructions had ceased to be understood, so the words upon the page lost meaning. Mere wriggling marks on paper, possibly an archaic set of symbols which might have meant something long ago. He turned his chair away from the pad on the table, and the curved top rail hit the wall.

If only he were able to obtain a dreamless, empty state, block out inner and outer semblance. All he could do was stare, sunken in the chair with his peaked cap crooked and a peculiar smile haunting his features. Perhaps there was mirth to be found in his situation, only it had not revealed itself as yet. He was prepared to believe that. There was no other reason for smiling. Indeed, every reason not to.

Clement experienced a surge of stamina as if he had been slapped across the face. He felt more in touch with reality than at any other time during the morning. He needed to stretch his legs. He wanted to inspect the offices in the building.

25

Umbrellas had blossomed in the distorted world beyond the revolving doors. Figure shapes moved past, appearing to Clement to be as ludicrous as their apparatus. And all had become anonymous grey. Sky overcast, raining grey distemper. Stone of buildings opposite, with their wavering awnings, had been stained to the hue of whitish slate. Cars were black or lighter shades of the same; indeed, every grey shape walking by wore grey overcoats or raincoats, and the clods of flesh which served for faces had been drained of colour. Clement was aware of the same process happening to him.

He was sure his blood had drained to his legs. He felt faint again. If only he had eaten at breakfast. For certain, if only he had eaten in the past few days.

Bringing up the insides of his wrists to rub his eyes, he accidentally knocked his cap and it fell to the carpet tiles. He let it stay there.

Like a fireworks rocket he had possessed a fierce energy for a duration but had quickly fizzled out. Unsure as to where he was going, he turned and staggered towards the lift then leant on a button.

The jaws of the lift rattled open and he fell inside. Slowly he slid down until his buttocks came to rest on the metal floor and he drew in his knees. With hands clasped around his ankles, he rested his chin.

At last he could achieve an unconscious state. There was no rush to move. The pose was reminiscent of his stay in the wardrobe the night before. This was important, he was convinced. Unclear as to how, only that this duplication of bodily posture in the cocoon was a significant element in his spiritual explorations. If only he had other elements, he could attempt to focus the energies of synchronicity and significant insignificance.

He pressed down upon his knees, his back sliding up a steel side of the lift, and stood upright.

Purely upon impulse, his hand reached out to a panel and he poked a button there, marked with the number two. The smokey button lit and with a squeak and a rattle, the lift doors closed.

He envisaged for a moment being trapped in this squeezing metal box, running around like any animal would in a cage; but then with a jolt, there was the sensation of movement and whining lift mechanism.

Another jolt, another pause, another hiss and rattle as the lift doors opened again.

Beyond the confines of the lift was a textured wall, brightly lit by lighting strips and lamps. A metal plate showed the floor number etched into its surface. Another exotic plant stood in its white tub on the corridor carpet. The red cylinder of a fire extinguisher stood guard further along the wall. The bouquet of cleaning fluids, hum of lights. Clement admired the view as though regarding a painting in a gallery but then the lift doors interrupted him and began to close. He jumped into the corridor with a nimble step.

The offices on each floor ran the length of the perimeter on four sides. He strolled casually, feeling important. He held his lapels and smirked. What responsibility he possessed, importance bestowed upon him for the honourable task of guarding this respectable building.

Each door to the offices was identical except for different digits upon it. He began to speak each office number as he went by as if it were a particular task he should perform.

After walking along two sides and while turning into the third, he stopped. Other than the shuffling as he brushed his blue nylon uniform, the soft padding of his feet on the carpet and the humming lights, there had been quietness. But then a feeling descended, quite unexpectedly, that someone was following. He turned rapidly to catch the intruder by surprise. The corridor was bright and empty.

He ignored the sensation, turned back and strode on, resuming the counting of numbers. 'Twenty-two – twenty-three…' he said, walking faster. He fought the temptation to turn again until reaching the end of the corridor.

If only he hadn't blinked he would have been certain: the edge of a jacket disappearing into an office – or the figment of a fraught imagination. He continued along the fourth side.

In another attempt to dismiss irrational feelings, he spoke the door numbers loudly and dwelled upon each one until fed the next. He performed mental arithmetic, either adding the two digits together or multiplying the two of them and doubling the result. Despite this effort, the feeling persisted. He must check all four sides again.

As he turned into the first corridor, walking past the lift, he was sure he had seen the sole of a tan brown shoe ahead before it vanished into the second corridor. Clement licked his lips and broke into a trot. He would capture the intruder.

With his mind set upon the task of pursuing the encroacher, numbers of the office doors seemed indignant at being ignored after his previous intimacy with them. They wished to be interfered with – they caught his eye and demanded again to be multiplied, divided or halved. Clement would glance up as he trotted by, catching number after number until his mind was crowded with a pack of them.

Cursing numbers, he turned the corner to see an elbow, just before it was pulled into one of the offices. There was no need to hurry now for he knew where to find the culprit.

He reached the office door, turned the handle, and pushed.

26

The two people within the office ignored Clement as he entered and sat at one of the leather topped desks. A large-framed man stood by another desk with his back to him, as well as to a young woman who had sidled up. She gave a polite cough while clutching office files. The man wheeled around from perusing over the town through the window, the sea glimmering in the distance.

'Ahh,' he let out with a show of teeth. 'The new secretary. Your name?' He put a sizeable hand to his cheek.

The woman unloaded the files onto his desk, already covered with the same. She appeared nervous and seemed unable to answer, and she gulped.

Miss Prim, Clement thought then.

'Miss Prim,' she answered in a quivering tone. Strands which had escaped from her bun of hair waved feebly, caught up by the suction of an extractor fan. The sun, pushing its way through vertical blinds, spread itself generously about the office; the distant roar of traffic emanating from below.

'No need to be nervous,' the man expressed encouragingly. 'Do your job well and I'm certain we will get along just fine. Who knows what bonuses you might be awarded?' A mild smile broadened to a leer. He held out his hand, the fat fingers littered with rings. 'Welcome to the company, Miss Prim. I am mister … mister…'

'Mr Proper,' called out Clement.

'Mr Proper,' said Mr Proper.

Miss Prim put her small hand within his. Hers were china-white and refined, contrasting with the ruddy backs and hairy knuckles of the other. She gave a curtsy and Mr Proper let out a laugh. 'Charming,' he said.

He indicated for her to be seated. And as she sat he did the same, nestling his bulk within a black winged chair behind his desk. They looked for a while, both waiting for the other to speak. A clatter of a typewriter came from one of the other offices. Clement noted the silhouette of a typist on the smoked glass of the adjoining office door. The handle of the door moved down but moved up again. He brought his attention back to the pair bathed in the hot sunlight, both waiting.

'Where did you work before?' muttered Clement.

'Where did you work before?' asked Mr Proper.

Miss Prim was tugging the edge of her dress over her knees while saying in a small voice, 'My previous job was in Edgington. I was a secretary there also. But for the past year while I've been married, I have not been working.'

Mr Proper appeared taken aback. 'A talented girl like you

with your secretarial qualifications, typing skills and such, and your beautiful hair, not working for a total of one year? Am I hearing correctly? Is this what you are telling me?'

Miss Prim was blushing. 'It's my husband, you see,' she answered, standing.

Clement leant forward to await the man's reply but he seemed unable to speak again. 'Perhaps he was right,' shouted Clement to prompt him. 'Perhaps your husband knows best. Perhaps you shouldn't have got this job, being so close to the pier.'

'Well, let me state,' Mr Proper was saying while walking over to a cupboard, 'I wholeheartedly agree with you. What a waste.'

Clement leaped to his feet and shouted, 'No, can't be right! What made you say that?' He went up to the executive who was changing the sober jacket of his suit for a brighter, striped one.

'What made you say that?' asked Miss Prim.

'Not the striped jacket, please,' pleaded Clement.

'Not the striped jacket,' agreed Mr Proper. 'Tell me young lady, where has the locket gone?'

Studying the girl's neck, Clement saw a green enamelled pendant hanging from a gold chain and sitting neatly in the cleft where her collar bones met.

'Where has the locket gone?' Clement also demanded.

She turned away. 'Leave me alone. I don't know why you make such a fuss.'

'Because I bought it for you, that's why. You're meant to wear it always as a symbol of my love. You said you would. You were going to put our photos in it or a lock of my hair. The chain's there – where's the gold locket gone?' Clement was standing close to her back and saw her shoulders rising and falling, and her hands to her mouth as though trying to stifle crying. But as he said, 'Look, I don't want to make you cry, I just want to know what happened to your present,' she turned about and it was obvious then she had been disguising laughter, her pretty face marred by a scornful expression.

'In my box on the dressing table, where do you think? Did you reckon I auctioned it, going to the highest bidder? A big drama over nothing.' She inspected her fingernails.

Clement went closer to her and spoke slowly, as if speaking to a child. 'Your keepsake. Tradition says you keep it with you always. It's a symbol.'

'A symbol of what? Of a birthday, that's what.'

'Of my love. I've already said. Where did you buy the grotesque lump in its place? Or has someone given it to you? You would rather wear jewellery from someone else? Am I right? What does a lump of rubbish symbolize?'

'You're talking utter rot,' she threw back. 'I don't know why it's so mysterious. I bought it in the mall, a couple of weeks ago. Just a cheap thing and I happen to like it.'

'I want you to wear the locket,' Clement demanded. 'Not much to ask, is it?'

Repeated abruptly from behind, 'Not much to ask, is it?'

Mr Proper furiously scribbled notes into a diary. He looked up and Clement considered that given a different light he might bear a passing resemblance to Dr Leibkov.

Clement went to speak to Bernadette again but she was no longer there. She had taken the sun with her; the dullness had returned. The sea of water on the horizon was now a sea of shabby buildings.

The adjoining office door was closing and he recognized the arm pulling it shut as belonging to Mr Proper. Then he heard Mr Proper's voice, identical to Dr Leibkov's, cry out, 'Bernadette! Come back, be as you were, please don't change.'

Clement ran over to the door and wrenched it open before running into the next office.

27

Mr Proper looked up while shuffling through pages of a thick file on his lap. 'Welcome, Donald. I am Dr Leibkov, your psychiatrist. Please, sit down.' Clement did as he was asked and was about to speak, when the doctor continued, 'We shall be seeing each other many times over the coming months. Our aim is fry your brain, possibly with onions and a mint sauce.'

'I see. What would this achieve?'

'Many things, occasionally alarming or tedious things, sometimes things with no picture. I'm quite adamant you will die.'

'You know I've brooded over death often. Doesn't frighten me though. On the contrary I find the prospect a fascinating one. I'll bide my time, however.'

'And why, when your vision of heaven is one of utmost perfection?'

'I wouldn't be able to keep my barriers because earthly possessions can't sully the heavenly kingdoms.'

The doctor appeared as if seen from a distance and

Clement quickly realised why: the doctor sat on the other side of an underground station platform within a wardrobe, tapping the beige file of papers with a pipe.

Clement stood as he felt warmth pushed out of the tunnel by an approaching train, a thrill beneath his ribs and strong invisible hands gripping his waist and holding him forward, a part of him goading, validating the compulsion to throw himself onto the track. The metal serpent roared out from its lair, lit carriages clanking past without stopping before being swallowed by the next tunnel ahead.

'Sit down, you're going too fast,' bellowed the doctor above the clamour and as Clement sat, Doctor Leibkov was before him again. 'Tell me more about these barriers.'

'They're as solid as you are there with your cynical expression, as relevant as the bowl of fruit on your desk. I can't lay a barrier onto your lap for you to stroke it like a cat yet is that proof of anything? Give me a lump of light wrapped in newspaper.

I've the understanding I may not be fully qualified to know for certain, though feel I'm closer to the truths than most.

For instance, are you able to recognize the melancholy of a steam train or see fundamental spirit-animal in real humans when eating? Not the ugly quivering jowls or the mouse-like nibbling. More the everyday consumption, where each bite is taken without conscious thought; the coy way in which eyelids slowly close before opening to chew the sustenance. Not many people would care to notice such minor details.'

'You are straying from the subject. You were a quiet, introspective youth.'

'Who told you this information?'

'That would be telling. Your manner acted as a foil to the garrulous ebullience of your friends. You were a mirror; you were blotting paper. You inherited worries. Shortly before your nineteenth birthday, this culminated in your refusal to leave your mother's house for three weeks. You persuaded your mother into perpetrating a lie on your behalf to the college.'

'How do you remember a lost memory?'

'This is your second appointment. Mother is most helpful in exposing the cracks. She thinks she is supportive. You know she's cruel. Drink your tea.'

Clement was startled when finding a cup and saucer in his hands. He tried to lift the teacup but found the simple task of transporting it impossible. No sooner had he curled his finger into the handle, there were mutterings and tuts from a host of unseen office workers. When he lifted the cup a matter of two inches from the saucer his hand and arm shook violently, making a quarter of the cup's contents spill onto the floor. A quaking ran up one arm and down the other. Neck muscles turned to a cold alabaster, solidifying against the spine. Stares were pricking his flesh and a light sweat broke out. Somebody gave a peal of laughter amidst the general murmur; he knew he had become the centre of attention again.

Spilling the tea, he felt, was as blasphemous and disgraceful as spitting in a church.

Then: 'Relax! Resolve to take hold of your destiny. Travel abroad, soak up life instead of misery, haggle over the price of fruit in sun-baked markets. Sip iced coffee at a hot street table, climb mountains, find adventures, write screenplays.'

'A decision is needed, yes. No howls of protest. Thick brushstrokes of a dream are sufficient, smaller details will paint themselves.'

'You remember your first job, don't you, in the shoe-mending shop?'

'I remember my first job in the shoe-mending shop. The buffer wheels, heavy leather smells mixed with lubricating fluids and polishes.'

'Busy, wasn't it? Constant traffic of customers. No sooner did you clear the counter of boots and shoes, then it'd be filled again with more. You'd put stretchers in them or pare the old heels ready for fresh ones.'

'During my lunch hour I'd go to a café and sit by the wall of mirror tiles to eat, watch reflections of customers. I began to recognize the regulars.

'Shoppers are in a holiday mood this morning. They move casually or lounge on benches scattered along the walkways and parades. A hum of chatter coming from the restaurant facing the piazza, overgrown umbrellas sprouting from the middle of tables shielding the patrons from the sun. And the sun is painting the awnings and terrace tiles, even the pensioners, in watercolour. Even the ugly clock tower squatting by the municipal fountain looks appealing, flooded by this pure light. It will give a tenor gong soon, to mark the hour. I notice pedestrians joining the queue which trails from the interior of the café.

'See that young woman over by the counter? I hadn't noticed her long hair until she stepped in. After leaving the sunshine in the street, still it possesses a natural auburn gloss. I've an urge to leave my stool and run over to stroke it.

'She might turn around to show her face. Do you think, despite the curving delineation of her body with that allure, she'll be wearing clumpy glasses on a misshapen nose, and have a surly mouth smeared with deep purple lipstick? I know differently.

'A car backfires from the high street like a gunshot. The hail of pigeons leaping up outside, their furious flurry of wings.

'She's turning. My pulse is a touch faster. What an appealing young woman, just as I remember.

'She turns back and is speaking quietly. The café assistant hasn't heard what she wants. Say again, he snaps impatiently. Because of my attentiveness I've understood her order. I'll shout it from my stool by the mirror tiles. Egg mayonnaise and cress. She'll half-turn this time — there we are. The assistant is just nodding, and preparing the sandwich. Quickly done, placing it into a bag, handing it over. She pays. She's leaving.

'I know it's wrong, but I must follow.

'She's walking towards a bench in the tree-lined square where the bristle-chinned hag feeds crumbs to pigeons. I walk over to sit next to my beauty; she regards me with surprise.

'Sorry I embarrassed you. That dopey bloke in the café must be getting a bit deaf.

'She's giving her coy smile and self-consciously taking a bite from her sandwich. I'm besotted with her.

'Nice day, do you think? And quite cold yesterday; wouldn't have reckoned on it, would you? Anyway, I suppose I'll get back to eating my plastic food. You here tomorrow? Yes, I will be. Great, I might be as well. Can I sit with you; eat our sandwiches together? Yes, that would be nice. Fine.

'I'll stand and walk away backwards, unwilling to take my sight from her. Tomorrow then. By the way, what's your name? Bernadette. Right, Bernadette, see you then. What's your job? Nosey, aren't I? Secretary. She suppresses a laugh. I've backed into a lamp post. Just my iceblink luck. Tomorrow, see you tomorrow! We wave.'

'I see.'

'I divulge another private memory and that's all you can say? I've explained meeting an amazing woman: not a plain, everyday beauty but a fusion of divinity; celestial, emanating compassionate warmth and loving ripples.'

Dr Leibkov wrote on a page in his folder, before saying, 'Your happy memories are of no concern to me. I need those which are protected, shielded from yourself. We need your barriers dissolving as easily as sugar in hot liquid, blacked-out mindrooms hidden in fathoms, exposed under a glaring spotlight.'

Each of the doctor's words had rolled and tumbled into the

next as skillfully as an acrobatic act.

Clement was so involved with internal mechanisms, eventually the office became insubstantial and as a lethargy washed through him, he ceased to sense anything but the mere ghost of being which resided within the clever construction of flesh and bone. Finally, his body was cast off completely as easily as discarding an overcoat. A rejoicing in temporary freedom, unencumbered by physical impediment.

He began a descent as though a diver swimming down to a mysterious and uncharted destination. While floating just below the surface he possessed sharp, darting ideas. Sinking lower he came across serious but colourful memories moving in a ballet, or more formal arrangements, swimming in large, ordered shoals within the indigo waters of his mind. Quirky concepts spun past or expanded and contracted in a peculiar way. As odd as they were, he was attracted to them. Lower still were the ponderous, skulking, difficult-to-see thoughts. Clement was glad of the ebony and thick cardinal blue, for some of the grotesque forms could have turned his sanity should he have seen them more clearly. Who knows what deformed and distorted monsters lurk in those lowest depths? Should even one of them be shown to light of the surface, they would surely grow to unimaginable size, able to feed off all else which swims there. Clement rose up and away with an urgency and gladly donned his body once more.

Moving slowly, holding a confusion as to his whereabouts, he went to the office door and wrenched it open, almost falling, staggering into and along the corridor.

The lift confronted him. He punched a button and the doors opened immediately. He lurched in; pressed for the ground floor; stood in a corner and waited there, breathing heavily while descending. Voices bellowing, the inner and outer worlds made of a shouting mania.

Back in the reception office, he finally became quiet within and relaxed. He had carefully rebuilt his barriers, locking particular mindrooms once more, ensuring they would never be opened again.

He was content having banished upsetting nonsense and false memories. How easy it would be to resist any mental attack, effortless to repulse ugly notions from him. 'If only the doctor understood,' he murmured, 'it would prove how normal I am."

He had asked the doctor once what he believed to be the definition of normality and had been amused to hear that the answer depended on one's viewpoint. Certainly, Doctor Smythe had answered, what is regarded as normal in one society is deemed abnormal in another. And time can change perspectives. Certain normalities of our century would not be applicable two centuries before.

Clement had interrupted. 'How you complicate, and yet you tell me not to do the same.'

He spoke those same words to himself again while watching his spectre reflection in the glass pane of the reception office.

He was contained within no other mental state other than normality. How could there possibly be anything wrong when he felt so ordinary, in complete control of his faculties?

There, before him, without a pause, the reflection continued to reproduce the tiniest of movement. While slowly closing an eyelid he saw the reflection performing the same. He lifted an index finger and opposite him the reflected finger was held up.

It was when he had closed both eyes and opened them quickly he noticed the reflection had followed a fraction of a second later. He tore his sight away, unable to sustain the communion any longer.

A minute more and he could have been trapped in the mirror of illusion as surely as his double had become.

28

Really do believe I'm able to stay here for always. Everything I need to sustain me. Lights when it becomes dark outside, heat from the electric fire. This savage heartbeat, given tempo and regulated by my orchestrated timepieces. I no longer feel hungry.

Perhaps there's a secret part of me which, now I no longer eat, will come into play. It will regulate metabolism for energies and bodily processes to be rationed, to maximize their potential. And maybe this vestigial capacity lies dormant in all real ones.

No need to see outside. I can create all I want with matchless clarity. If I pluck these organs out from their sockets it wouldn't matter. Here, I have it clearly: the clothes shop with its awning and awkward mannequins, next to the butchers. I'll wave to the butcher while he stands by trays of red and mottled meats. His head shall be that of a turkey, the wattle hanging obscenely from below its beak, bright comb flattened under a straw hat.

A green lorry has moved into view and blocked my perception of him. Only his gobbling instructions can be heard. But what an advantage I have over normal vision. The butcher now unseen by me – the perceiver – no longer exists. You understand, doctor?

That lorry, painted such a gaudy emerald. The colour's evolving to chlorophyll paste and if I regard it much longer, I'll become nauseous. My attention will stay on the two strongmen, seagull-moustached, dressed in tiger skins, standing on the back of it. Able to lift the barrels of tar and bags of cement, and lead caskets of pristine elastic bands. There are boxes and crates stacked neatly at the back of the lorry. They should contain, if I'm not much mistaken, bottles of musk oil and hair clips. The crowds are dawdling over those curling pavement slabs, each holding hands with the next.

I should be able to construct a whole sphere of existence, tuning each element to perfection.

Another question begs an answer. Doctor, you might know. You will be coming out of the library. Look over here, the least we can do is wave to each other.

Admit my power. I've made you and I can control you, much in the same way as you would want with me.

Three students, A, B and C, with crooked caps and uninfected vision, by your feet, will shuffle along to allow you to pass. They are studying graphite constructs with protractors and set-squares.

But listen, you're walking too fast.

Will you wait for me to catch up? What strength of character you own which enables you to defy your creator.

There we have it. I've touched upon the crucial question I spoke of. Are you listening to me, doctor?

'I am,' you can say. 'Any problems you have can be problems shared.'

'I know, and I'm grateful. I've had much weight on my mind lately.'

'Where am I, Donald?'

'I've made us a cobbled street in a village. We are next to the police station over to the west, with the chimes of a big bell striking. Maybe not – let it be a park with neat flowerbeds and impeccable lawns of rolling exquisiteness. Distant birdcalls are from macaws and plumed parrots, with the shrieks of peacocks. I'll have a peacock strut past for us, opening and closing its eye-speckled tail like a huge fan.

Let's sit here on this bench overlooking the lake. The face of the water has copied the sky for its decoration. See the toy boats floating lethargically amongst the lily pads on its glass surface?'

'You are in danger of straying from the subject again. I can only help if you try to help yourself. One must decide; you must cultivate self-discipline. I understand it might seem harsh sometimes but that is as you would want, I remind you. This aspect came out strongly from our first meeting together.'

'I wonder to myself – more at night, kept awake by a mind wound up like the mainspring of an alarm clock which won't run down – I think if I'm ever going to be as I was. I must clutch your arm. This sensation of being in free fall without moving has become part of me.'

'Indeed, hold on. You are in the grip of vertigo.'

'Thank you, I'm feeling quickly better. Passes as fast as a gust of air. If only—' How quickly you interrupt.

'Your question. Ask me this question which is upsetting. You need information.'

'I need to be told: God is creation yet in spite of this I'm able to create a world just as valid as It, although I'm no god. How can this be?'

'Your words are based on the false assumption that there is a reality which may exist in your mind, as relevant as the one known through our senses. Why continue to clutter your life with such notions?'

'Who's side are you on? Since I've been visiting, doctor, there've been so few times when you've agreed with me. What are you becoming? Untrue? If only you'd try to understand. The usual life is full of deceit and lies; it's sham. Not really what it seems or pretends to be. Even this particular mindroom is false: the flowers here have been created out of an extruded plastic; wood of this park bench manufactured from a synthetic material; the machinery used to produce these falsehoods is false. Certainly the imposters have a degree absolute of falseness in them. Their appearances are masks to hide the true feelings beneath. Faces unknown – who can be trusted? I no longer know.'

'You'll learn to trust again. One must have a balanced view. It is as bad to trust everyone and everything as to distrust all.'

'If only I am able to encompass this fully and grow with the concept though I'm unable to accept it. I've lost ability to distinguish between real from not real in this case; unable to extract lies from truth like a mental dentist.'

'But this is why you are here. We will find truth together. Your faith has been shaken. But it's not beyond redemption. You must face reality. First you have to prepare for hurtful emotions. Tell me about your ex-wife.'

'I don't wish to talk about her, my wife; I still haven't repaired fully.'

'Do you not remember getting divorced?'

'Do you remember dredging up the same old vile lies? Leave me be to consolidate, please. There have been too many copies, false ones, poisoning her beautiful perfection. How you are falling for that, is beyond me.'

'What if Bernadette wasn't perfect? I could suggest the phrase "putting someone on a pedestal". You understand that analogy? Do you think there's a bit of that?'

'Are you a woman hater?'

'Of course not. I'm merely trying to find the truth, not for me, but for you.'

'I'll tell you the truth. Men are out of touch with those vibrations perceived by women, the profound receptacles, conduits from a mysterious spiritual realm to being here.'

'Most poetic, Donald, but how does that have relevance to

Bernadette?'

'For an intelligent man, you can say the stupidest of things. Women are incorruptible; they are the lovers of truth and peace, loathers of deceit.'

'And yet Bernadette hid truth, from you. I have it here, in my notes; this is what you told me on Thursday. How did she deceive you, do you think? Are you deceiving yourself because you know the answer but won't accept it?'

'She used words as weapons, that's all. How could she have ever meant what she said? She would never betray me. We love each other. Don't we?'

29

'**Y**ou won't answer.'

'To be honest, I'm fed up with you constantly using that phrase. Think of another record to play.' She is taking tomatoes from her shopping bag and placing them on the work surface by the sink. 'Donald!' she cries out unexpectedly. Let me replay it: 'Donald!' I don't recognize my own name. 'You've left the milk out again.'

'Really, why worry?'

I'll snatch at the carton and will accidentally knock a mug. There I go. And there it goes, skittering across the work surface. Hits the bread bin. Handle broken off and a wedge dropped from around the rim. Puddles of cold coffee in streaks on the worktop.

'Imbecile, look what you've done. My dad bought me that on the pier.' She's picking up the pieces.

I'm feeling sheepish. 'I'll buy you a new one.'

'Won't be the same, will it.'

'I really am sorry.' I'll go to hold her.

'Get off. Forget it. Get out of my kitchen.'

'No need to get into a mood. How can you expect me to respect you with an attitude like that?'

Watch her turn as she holds the pieces over the bin; see her stare in a peculiar way; wet pottery dripping.

'Who cares about respect?' Such a spiteful tone. 'I don't respect you anyway, why should I worry?'

'What are you trying to do? You really have changed. It hurts to hear you being nasty. We're meant to discuss, expose our innermost feelings. Instead, you keep secrets.'

She has disposed of the broken mug. Pushing me aside she snaps, 'Give it here, useless,' and pulls the carton of milk from me and puts it into the fridge. 'Can't be expected to tell you everything. Who are you to demand? I'm sure you've got your secrets, anyhow.'

'No I haven't. At least, not from you.'

Squirt of washing-up liquid into the bowl. Her hands are in the sink to wash dishes, the cutlery rattling. 'Like hell. For instance, how many times have you been unfaithful?'

The casual way she asked this. 'Never be unfaithful. You must know that, surely.'

'Oh, do I?' She places a washed plate on the draining board. My sight has come to rest on her hair clip. 'You might have been in a situation which was difficult to get out of. It can happen, thoughts of those girls where you work, for instance.'

'This is ridiculous. Alright I admit, that's natural, merely in my old imagination.'

'Listen' – near to a whisper, sounding mischievous – 'tell me how many affairs you've had then I'll tell you how many I've had.'

Anguish building up inside, an aggravating influence.

'I've never. I really can't see why you're talking like this.' I'll spin this pretender about to face me. Soapy hands are limp to her sides. Her eyes, showing coldness, looking at mine, her head turned away. 'Tell me what you mean. Are you saying you've had an affair?'

She's grinning the more, making fun of me. Of course my pretty young wife wouldn't have committed adultery. This version is hurting with words. Her falsehoods are to punish me for breaking her mug, I can understand that.

I must try to pull her closer, but she's struggling in my grasp. And without warning, she's gone and in her place is you, doctor. Don't you see my furious frustrations? Anyway, who have I been talking too? One of you is illusory. You've easily tricked me to reveal another part of myself buried, a false filmic protected from ever being seen again.

Try telling me once more to trust and I might spit in your face. All it brings is confusion and sadness. And even these are not what they seem, being no more than electrical activity and chemical reaction. They can't be regarded in any other way. I feel despair but also comprehend there really is no such emotion. Nor is there sadness, happiness or misery.

I won't believe in your world. And I'm starting to distrust my own. If that fails, I'll be taken down to nothing.

30

It was dusk. Street lamps threw orange glare over wet pavements. No longer was it raining though a brisk coldness ran freely along the streets. Few pedestrians went quickly by, holding coat lapels up to their ears or burying raw mouths into scarves. A light came on above the clothes shop and curtains were hurriedly drawn. Then, pushing out a silver-buttoned uniform in an indifferent defiance to the cutting breeze, a policeman strode by. His cheeks glowed more red than seemed natural (as red as coals in the hot chestnut brazier on the corner of Market Street) as though he had applied dabs of rouge to either side of his nose. He kept on course, forcing an approaching couple to unlink. A paper bag overtook all three and hopped along the road as though pulled by an invisible thread before flying up, then lodging finally in one of the gutters piping the roofs.

A man bent down to tie a shoelace. Once this task was accomplished, he turned his head towards the lit foyer.

Clement had switched off the light in his office some time

before. He had become aggravated by passers-by staring in. The action of one rude person seemed to stimulate another. Clement was becoming a trained observer, able to decide who would want to make him the observed before they looked.

His breath quickened with vexation. Pedestrians, one after the other, entered quickly and filled up the quadrants of the revolving door as if flies attracted to flypaper. The door now revolving, around and around, like a merry-go-round, to the music from a fairground organ.

Clement turned away, feeling bilious.

He ached, and grunted with the painful effort of bending down to a filing cabinet under the counter. He pulled open the bottom drawer and took out four newspapers from it and a roll of adhesive tape. The newspaper would have to be a substitute for tin foil.

He sat by the small table for a while, attempting to regain composure.

'The doctor is clever,' he said. The distinguished man had been cunningly chipping away his resistance as patiently as a stonemason. Clement sensed other enemies of the barriers coming closer, rallying with a hideous whispering, a manic scuffling. His defenses were failing. And apprehension was growing. He must make himself safe against two foes, he felt, not only from attacks within but also an invasion of privacy from without. A protected domain needed to be built, a realm which would exclude others. Another cocoon.

He was ready. He went into the foyer and began to cover

the window glass of the reception office exterior with sheets of newspaper, neatly and methodically, his back to the attentive audience trapped in the revolving doors. Each spread of newsprint overlapped the next and every edge carefully stuck with a layer of tape. After more than a third of the pane had been covered, the sense of being watched became overwhelming, forcing the decision to continue from within the office.

When he had covered three quarters of the window, the strip lighting and spotlights from the foyer were barely adequate to work by. He thought to switch on the reception office light again or keep the door open but decided against these options, instead waited a while for his eyes to adjust.

The job of covering the window pane was complete. Without even a glance to admire the finished work, he turned to the back wall and pulled away the table and chair from it. A calendar and a date planner were ripped down with impatience; time was not to be wasted. He was developing an enthusiasm which quickened the pulse. He pulled his left shoe off.

The first blemish to the wall would have been an accident. Mr Klipps might have leant too heavily in his chair, causing the back of it to strike the plaster, making a centipede of a crack. This effect repeated many times, enough for a small piece of the plaster to fall, leaving a hole for bare brick to show through.

Clement went to it and using the end of his pencil to poke into the hole, attempted to make it larger. He had the idea he would like to sketch a picture on the blank expanse but rejected the thought without much consideration. Using the sole of his shoe as a hammer and the pencil as a chisel, he proceeded to chip away more of the plaster. The pieces were tiny and the job time-consuming. He swore under his breath when, after his shoe struck the end of the pencil at an oblique angle, the writing instrument snapped into two, sending splinters to the dusty pile along the skirting.

He should find proper tools. But before this he must be in league with Donadette again, he decided; the lively and modern, sexless and kind-thinking Donadette on this occasion who would prefer heavy, expressive makeup to enliven a cultured face. Apart from that, the stubble of his beard needed to be disguised.

He undressed and put on the blouse and skirt taken from his holdall. When applying the makeup, he attempted to match his own movements with the peculiar animated reflection – spattered with print – showing in the window glass. So be it, he decided. He used the lipstick to draw runes and hieroglyphs, spirals and intimately-crossed lines; first on his palms and wrists, then on the glass. Words on the newspaper caught his attention. He applied mauve cross-hatching to some while circling others, such as "multifoiled", "Phaedra", "porcupine", "tree" and "kookaburra".

When ready, and not bothering to return the shoe to his

foot, he pulled open the door and went back into the foyer. Crowds had gathered outside. They stood motionlessly, watching him with blank expressions. Those standing within the partitions of the revolving door had their faces distorted, pushed hard to the glass panels.

Clement had no time for them. An important mission had been bestowed.

31

He took the steps down to the basement in twos. There were bound to be tools there, he was convinced.

Once he had checked in the cupboards by the stairwell – finding only cleaning equipment – he opened the metal entrance to the basement.

Immediately a sickly heat embraced his face and neck. Sweat began to run down his back. Heavy steam filled the room and erased details.

Clement went further in until he saw the large outline of the boiler. The dials were alive as the needles within them quivered and flicked. As he observed with a puzzled awe, the boiler's studded curves of metal turned from copper to bronze, from bronze to red, from red to flamingo pink. If he were to touch the surface of the boiler it would burn the flesh from the bone, he knew. He undid the top button of his blouse and loosened the leather belt of his skirt before wiping a hand across his brow. He had become soaked as if from a thrown bucket of water. A rumbling came from the metallic cylinder, an ominous growling, and one which filled Clement with a sense of foreboding. The pipes along the walls shook and rattled and let out spurts of steam.

He must take action before it was too late. But what to do: stop the flow of water, oil, or bovine blood for all he knew? If only he had become technically-minded.

There, near a corner, was an open toolbox containing a hammer and chisel. He ran to it but was stopped by a figure emerging through the billowing masses of swaddling steam.

'Won't be long. Nobody can stop it. It's going to blow up.' The boilerman had made these remarks before wiping a greasy hand across his green overalls. His other hand released a wrench and it clattered onto the concrete floor.

Clement asked with growing fear and trepidation, 'How much longer before it's destroyed?'

'Well, it depends of course.' The figure stood by one of the twitching dials and put his palm upon it without reaction. 'A few factors are involved.'

'Like what? You've got to tell me. I demand it. I'm the security guard here and I've a responsibility to this dream building. It's essential I'm told pertinent details concerning maintenance and upkeep of the place. It really is your duty to speak.'

The boilerman was shaking his head slowly. 'Certainly I would say if I knew myself. But I don't, you must understand. The only fact I'm privy to? It's going to go, but I'm unable to tell you when.'

Clement took a step towards the man but he also took a step, standing before the sweltering boiler, covering himself with the white steam clouds.

Clement's pleading tone, officialism gone forever: 'How do we stop it? How can it be stopped?'

'I have no means to stop it. But you have, Donald. Your ability is enough. The solution has always been with you.'

'Please, I'm begging you. I've seen too much already. Allow me these last barriers.' He sank to his knees and held his hands up, locked tightly together as though in prayer.

'It cannot be. Tell me, while we have the chance, while you can save yourself; save all of us.'

Clement sniggered. How stupid he had been! 'You were close to succeeding this time,' he shouted out, triumph in his voice, standing again. 'I can see through you, as easily as if you were a gas. Then that's what you are, not even solid. How can a mere puff of steam tell me what to do? You're a vision. Yes, it's thundered back; I recall. It is I who have created you. Without me, you wouldn't be. You're part of an extraordinary dream which I've not left behind. How close I came to falling into your crafty trap! Listening to a phantom, a creation from my cerebellum only. I could have succumbed to your trickery, and told you all.

'Though lend an ear, Mr Nobody – I'm a fair man. I can tell you another story if it's your wish. And if I relate it, will you be satisfied? I have my doubts.

'This dream of mine seemed to have come about abruptly.

They do, don't they? It must have had a definite start at some time or other. I had been plunged into it as quickly and unexpectedly as falling over a cliff. But when this was, I can't say. And I find myself still trapped. As a dreamer, I have no recollection of ever being awake.

'Listening carefully, gaseous nothingness?

'It felt as though I had been crying though don't remember doing that. Such realism was portrayed that I actually felt cold.

'I walk along a country road in the middle of the night, in my underwear. Vivid, utterly realistic. I believe this is called an anxiety dream. Either side of the road stretches unlit countryside under a depressing dome. I'm in the grip of claustrophobia. But how can one escape from the confines of an open road? I can see myself trying to become awake. I've since given up, I might add. There's only a morbid dread of awakening anyway, as I have this idea I'll wake up into another dream. A dream within a dream, like Russian dolls – for every pained dream existence, another to enclose it.

Coldness had affected my bladder. I can remember stopping to pee in a ditch before continuing this night journey.

'Staggering as though drunk. The wind is high and blowing me about as easily as if I were a spinning top. I'm having to walk at a sharp angle to combat the charge of it. Innards are churned up. A dire draining sickness which has concealed itself inside. I neither know where I've come from nor where I'm going.

'There are times when a nightmare can wrench at your

arteries for you are unaware it's a dream state. Here, with the knowledge that all which might occur is an illusion, does help. Though not much as I seem to be feeling even colder. I'm beginning to sob, not from the effects of the spiteful wind but because of a monumental welling up.

'Another element occurring. A car has picked me out in its headlights, and has stopped. The driver seems shocked. Perhaps it's because I'm wearing underpants only and I've no shoes on, and my feet are bleeding.

'Teeth are chattering so much I can barely speak. He asks me where I live, given me a blanket. The heat from under the dashboard is sheer bliss. For some reason I don't want to go home. I give the address of Penshart Press. He drives on, asking questions as if he might be a doctor, but I don't listen.

'Although much warmer in the car, claustrophobia has captured me again and is manipulating my emotions as easily as if I were a ball of plasticine. Trapped within this confined, stifling space, I need to tell this man of a tragedy. I have overwhelming feelings but can't recall what calamity has happened.

'The fiction becomes hazy at this point when I dreamed I was dreaming. Huge sets of grinding wheels and dentist drills hammer my teeth; falling from a plane and landing on a gargantuan woman, being drowned by her hot mountains of flesh.

'Complete gaps in this fantasy of the night. I vaguely remember an argument. Then waking up to a surprisingly strong early morning sun, lighting the interior of the gate cabin. The door is ajar and a group of people are staring in, calling my name.

'There, in detail, capturing every nuance of their character, is old Herbert the gateman, along with Stones and Sylvia. They're acting in a serious manner. I have the impression there's an important matter in hand. Without warning, many pairs of hands lifting me and wrapping me in more blankets. These men are wearing uniforms. And I understand why, when I'm carried to a stretcher on wheels. An ambulance awaits. I wasn't aware of being ill. A police car as well, with one of the policemen talking to Stones. Imposters, for certain.

'I could tell more of this dream but it might bore you. What am I saying. How can someone who doesn't exist become bored?

'My imagination is faultless. Aspects of hospital I included were truly inspired. And it's there, in that unreal place, where I created my piéce de resistance.

'No less than you, Dr Leibkov, in all your borrowed glory. I really should retain modesty but I must say your apparent cleverness has been nothing other than belonging to me.'

The doctor stepped closer to Clement, waving the billows of steam from his path. There was no need to hide, his identity revealed.

'You have given a convincing case, Donald. I'm impressed. But you must believe in me as real. If I am unreal, I'm still part of you. To destroy me would be to destroy a piece of yourself. And what you have told me is not enough. Observe the effect of your stubbornness.'

Still the boiler was grumbling and glowing pink though as Clement watched, it was turning white hot. His composure was disrupted again and panic took hold.

He spoke rapidly: 'I must trust myself, even if there is nobody else to trust. Then it follows that if you are me then I must trust you? I hope so. I've been deceived much in life. But isn't it enough I've already given, against my wishes? Obviously not, for the boiler is complaining louder. The end could be near. Distant noises as if from horses' hooves of an unstoppable cavalry. Soon an explosion will occur which would rip us apart.

'Is this no worse than opening more secret mindrooms and unleashing false memory? That'll tear at me as surely as any explosion. I would be spoilt, violated. Reduced to dehypnotized toothpaste probably; be without solidity, without function. I've tried telling you this, doctor, but you've become conveniently deaf. I would be shredded.

'The final barriers have begun to be chipped away. It's only a matter of time. The void awaits.'

32

How can a city without substance still beat a dull, humdrum existence? Sounds of the occasional car moving over glistening roads, or braying voices of the full-bellied as they postulate on the steps of the restaurant: it's so convincing, here in my hushed mind. It has a strong will to exist but I refute it. All has been rightly condemned and is simply no longer there. Space has curved in on itself with me at its centre. If I were to walk out through the doorway I would find myself where I had started, the door behind and this chisel rasping at blisters.

I'm finding this serious labour cathartic. Rid the brickwork of its carapace. Satisfying when decent chunks fall, like that. I suspect there's dampness in the wall caused by a break in the damp course. You wouldn't know such details, being a doctor. Building regulations aren't part of your training. But then, an architect isn't interested in sucking brains dry, as you do. Just because you remain silent doesn't mean I can't feel your presence. You're overseeing the work like a foreman. It's as though this wall covering is a mindroom, isn't it? I'm not stupid, I do understand the principles. Tell me I'm wrong but as I hack at the wall you are behind my back hacking at barriers. Already a dribble of make-believe memories is seeping through a crack you've made. You might as well listen, seeing as you're the cause. Let me construct and project them onto these bricks and plaster.

The living room is empty for a while as if a stage waiting for its players. A meaningful suspense can mount. Pristine elastic bands of anticipation can vibrate as high as violin strings. How well the lighting crew have worked to create the impression of a morning sunlight radiating through the front windows.

With the next blow from the hammer onto the chisel, this fake play will begin…

'Aren't you ready yet?' She's calling up the stairs, her lips, bright with lipstick, puckered with annoyance. 'If you're not ready by the time he comes then just you wait.'

I'm pulling my jacket on as I come down. 'And what's that meant to mean?' Walk around her to the kitchen for a drink of water. Surely there's water in the tap.

She's following.

'You haven't got time. He'll be here soon. He's going to be punctual, which is more than I can say for some people. And comb your hair, you look like a scarecrow.'

'Not even two o'clock yet. And what do you expect my wig to look like with this dust?' Without thinking, I've gone to the kettle to fill it. 'I don't really want us to go anyway. What's this about?'

I've returned to the living room.

'I don't know what you mean. It's about us going out for a change. I think it's a good idea.'

'Yes, but I'm not keen on anyone else coming along. Why can't it be just the two of us, the two of us, the two of us?'

'Well for a start, we haven't got a car.'

'And why? Because this Aaron bought it, that's why. We could catch a bus.'

'And where do we catch a bus at one in the morning?'

The stage tipping from side to side like a boat on the sea. 'What do you mean one o'clock? You said the party was in the Neptune Hotel. The bars close after eleven.' Feeling upset; too shaky. I'll start on the patch of plaster to the right.

'It's a private party, stupid. There's an extension.'

Don't call me stupid, Binny. For goodness sake, can't we call this off?'

She's gazing through the French windows to the back garden. Waves lap the patio. 'And don't call me Binny.' In a louder tone, 'No thought of what I want. Anyway, it's Aaron's favour. You don't want to appreciate it. We've got to go.'

A pattern which I recognize, like a script practiced for the past two days, is beginning to emerge. I sit but stand again straight after. Nerves are jangling. If only I could relax and calm down.

'There's no "got to" about it. We can apologise when he

arrives and tell him we can't make the day or the party. Then I'll take you somewhere nice, just us. What do you say?'

She has spun around quickly. 'No,' she answers with her antagonistic posture, hands on hips. 'I've promised him.'

'You really can't see how this is hurting me, can you? This person coming between us – who does he think he is?'

'You're being pathetic again, Donald. He's not coming between us. He's a friend, as I keep on telling you. He's got a girlfriend, if it helps. She's coming as well.'

'I couldn't give a damn. I've told you, I don't want to meet him again and I'm certainly not interested in meeting any of his girlfriends.'

'Any of my friends either then. You make it like I'm not allowed any friends of my own. You might as well live in the Middle Ages.'

Blood pounding in pulses in my neck. This argument is an eternally spinning wheel which, by centripetal force, we can never escape from. The chisel will take a heavier blow but it won't lessen my giddiness. I've no choice but to reveal my rampant jealousy and shout back, 'As long as your friends are girls. Why men, why this Aaron? You're married. I don't see why you need him.'

She has gone to the front window when she hears a car's engine but it's only the neighbours leaving for the shops. 'Because I find him interesting,' is her answer. 'Because my life is getting boring.'

There's the danger this argument will flare into a raging

fight. But with my comment of, 'So you think I'm boring, yes?' Bernadette simply snorts.

How she taunts me! See, see the sun creating the silken rays about her, stroking an immaculate complexion, dancing within her stunning locks, defining her curvaceousness within the tight skirt and black stockings. She glows with an inner strength, one which she has stolen from me.

Although I had put the locket back on its chain for her to wear again, I've noticed – as she runs fingers through her untied hair – the enamel pendant is still with her, dangling from her bracelet. I want to rip it off and stamp on it. Still I despise it and all it might stand for. But my suspicions are only unreal monsters, I must believe that.

'Maybe I have become boring.' Waves of sentiment and self-pity washing over me. I wish for her to see my softness of emotion then she might soften herself. 'I understand I haven't been taking you out much. I can make it up to you, you know — and as for the car…'

'He's here!' she shouts gleefully and I'm feeling physically sick.

33

Let me mark the end of this first act with a significance, perhaps synchronicity – the final clout from the hammer which will cause the last of the plaster to come from the first wall.

There, blow by blow, I've hacked away. I must stand back to admire it though not for too long. Time is hunched like a lewd and malicious demon, a task-master urging me forward with outrageous remarks muttered into my ear canal. I've no choice but to continue, here on the second wall.

The stink is unbearable. Can't anyone else smell it?

'As usual…'

'I'm being stupid, I know,' I finish for her.

'Not that stupid,' remarks Aaron. I'm irritated by his support of me. 'It's Syd the fish man, up there,' and he indicates to the inside of the chalet door as though we can see through it down the length of the pier. 'Dumps his waste bags at the side.' The handsome smile from beneath his moustache is annoying.

'Shouldn't do that,' says Bernadette. 'It might spoil your bike.'

'His as well. I've told him time and again not to lean it here. I'm thinking you'd fancy a bike ride.' He's suspiciously even-toned.

Bernadette making a weird ticking noise with her tongue.

You've been forced too close in the cramped quarters of the chalet. My skin is twisting in knots. 'Let's leave. We can go somewhere to eat.' Let out hurriedly, trying not to show anxiety.

'Not yet, Donald. Aaron's going to read my palm again. He really is good. He'll do yours, if you like.'

Where has the sharpness gone? Her cutting tone has been successfully cultured over the past three months but with this dire man here, it's gone. Her voice has become a graceful timbre again, softly-spoken.

'I don't want my damned palm read.'

Aaron has taken hold of Bernadette's hand and gently unfolding her fingers. She has her eyes wide and they shine like a minor presented with sweets; and she's giving that particular smile which used to belong to me only.

'Fair enough,' she replies quietly as he intently examines the lines on her exposed palm.

I want to wrench her hand away despite knowing it would appear a fatuous act. I could walk out but this would leave them together. How have I managed to get this far into a situation which I didn't want? I should be more firm. I should have ordered. Seems to be the only way.

Aaron has brought his head up with its mop of black hair and says, in a positive and confident manner, 'A strong love line.'

His smile again, honest and wide; any insinuation, evaporated. What impertinence — but I'll not be pressured into retaliation, except the hammer pounding the chisel with contempt. Some might say I should raise my voice or fists, but this won't be my way. The destruction of this man who would try to steal my wife will be surreptitious; he'll be unaware of its progress. She can only ignore him and come to me with admiration and respect when she sees how reasonable I've become. Again I will be warmed with her love. He'll be maimed with laughter, scalded with wit, finally destroyed with my goodnaturedness.

I'll return a smile, add a chuckle even. Did I detect his face whitening a little? Perhaps not – however, eventually he'll crumble before us, Bernadette no longer under his spell.

For the while I must be patient. My time will come. I'll hide vengefulness, be composed, exude only a venomous serenity.

Hit the wall and the stones they come a-tumbling-down. My blouse and skirt are covered in dust. I'm sure the agency will understand once I've explained. They might be waiting outside on the pier.

A line of seagulls preening themselves, perched on the railings. Women have taken off their bonnets in common respect for the important agency instructors. Now we've come out of the chalet onto the boards, the agents hide, satisfied to watch us from a distance.

How neat and tidy everyone is, and here I am in mucky clothes.

Strike the wall.

'Pleased to meet you.' Said to Lucy, even though I'm not. Immediately I sense an aspect of this girl which I dislike. Can't quite understand what – she appears reasonable enough, dressed in a light frock with strawberries printed on it, white socks and sandals. She's attractive as well, even with too much makeup and the clutter of imitation diamonds about her person.

'Well,' Lucy says and surprising me by taking my arm, 'Where will we whistle off to? Anywhere exciting?'

'We could go for a quick bite in the cafeteria. Then we really must make a move.'

Bernadette frowning. 'Don't be silly, Donald. Why did you say that?'

Why did you say that? Why did you say that?

I must grit my teeth to stop from speaking further. She's liable to make me seem a fool. I'm already embarrassed: neck has become stiff and hot, and I'm feeling a mild blush in my cheeks as scrutiny has come to me.

Lucy cries out, 'Let's go on the rides,' and she's pulling; I'm thrown off-balance and as my hand leaves a pocket, her fingers have quickly entwined with mine and she's tugging me along the pier towards the funfair. She's surprisingly strong.

'I don't really want to go.' How feebly I muttered that. All she does is pull me the more.

Bernadette calling over, 'See you in twenty minutes.' I turn around in time to see her linking with Aaron and strolling arm in arm back to the chalet.

I have to shout, 'No, wait.' It should serve a dual purpose, for not only do I want my wife back here, I also need this nimble girl to cease her continual pulling of my arm.

Old ladies licking ice creams, bunched together on those covered benches – handbags on laps – and fishermen in their deck-chairs, giving me disapproving stares.

But will nobody stop them? Certainly not those fishermen: one of them has climbed onto the railings and thrown himself off. 'Knit one, plain one,' an elderly citizen mutters as explanation, with clicking from her knitting needles.

I've managed to pull free from Lucy and I'll march towards the chalet. Bernadette has gone inside. Thump the hammer. Feeling the blows in my chest. Aaron has stepped up to the chalet interior. My anxiety has me almost whimpering. Another four yards and I'll be there. The slatted door has closed. I must get there before … before what?

Lucy has come up behind and put her arms around my waist. I must struggle to free myself from her but she's tittering as though I'm playing a game.

'Come on, you dappy man. They'll be alright. Aaron likes to read palms.'

'Well he might but he doesn't have to do it in that crappy shed.'

'But that's what it's for. Don't worry, they won't be long.'

I'll shriek out as if I've discovered a secret formula, 'I've remembered: he's read her palm already; there's no need for them to be in there.'

Smash the wall.

Can you see what's happening here, doctor? See what you're making me uncover?

As inevitable as the destination of the roller coaster, along with the excited squeals of its passengers. Once started there's no stopping and it must roll on to the end.

My flesh is burning. I'm ill with worry. Lucy is giggling now. I understand the aspect of her I dislike. She appears shallow; I doubt she could be serious for more than a minute.

Clout the hammer, expose brickwork hiding guiltily beneath the plaster.

Please, don't pull me away. I must open that door. My wife is inside; can't you understand? Don't you hear me screaming? I'm unable to put them into words, you would think me disturbed. Strangely, these screams from inside as I hit the chisel, they're coming from the single seagull circling above, its cries beginning to resemble a siren.

Watch how it attacks the chalet. Believe me, I have no effect on its actions. Though I must be honest I'm urging it on as it spins in large arcs before flying at speed to the door — but then plunging back into the suffocating air at the last moment.

I can't see anything else but the chalet suspended in sky as this gull attacks it in frenzied waves.

Possibly I'm partly responsible for the bird. Each hammer belt at the end of the chisel – every time a lump of chalky plaster joins the piles – this gull begins another descent to the chalet. And the chalet, I can't rid it from view. I've encompassed it, fumbling over its boarded surface like an insect twitching antennae. This is becoming a nightmare. My nose is pressed onto the wood; I'm reeling.

Sent away from the sealed chalet entrance, wrapped in squealing elastic bands.

Hammer blow after hammer blow.

Before I'm ready, sent hurtling back towards the chalet, propelled at an unnatural rate. Slow down or I'll slam into it; stopped abruptly, once more nose pressing hard up to the boards. Squeezing tears from between my burning eyelids. My cheeks are scratched.

Blow after blow.

I've been roughly pulled again, away from this structure. Must I spend the rest of my life thrown backwards and forwards with this loathsome nausea turning my whole body into squeaking sponge?

'You'll make me sulk in a minute,' says Lucy, tightening her grip about my waist.

See the chalet, as flat as a painting, becoming as grey as plaster. The sky's surface has been blemished by the chisel prising away parts of it.

'To the funfair,' the seagull demands as though it were a trained parrot; Lucy's begun pulling again.

'Lucy, no, we must … we must…' but already I'm weary and resigned to go with her. I might as well be a puppet with its strings cut. Muscles inflamed and taut. Throat sore; legs have lost feeling from crouching down for too long; I've a harassing ache in my groin area.

Please, Bernadette, you must come out of there. If you must hide, hide in the wardrobe, in the cocoon. You've been inside for ten minutes.

'Here, Donald—'

Where are you hiding? Show yourself. You're close. Over there, by the amusement hall or in the doorway of the cafeteria? Be seen. Maybe you've gone down to the beach, sitting by the sea sifting sand, collecting shells. Or you might be under this pier, swinging your legs as you sit on one of those huge, mollusc-covered struts.

'Over here.'

Still can't see where. The rest have walked on ahead. They're too fast. At least stop for a short while. Remember how weary I am. The weight of the hammer has doubled. I can barely lift it more than a foot. Can't bring it hard down onto the end of the chisel, just let it fall. Look at this blister on my thumb: have you ever seen one quite so large? If I were to pierce it with a pin, the pus would spurt out.

'Here, here I am.'

Stop playing games. Let me catch up. Wait where you are.

I must rest for a few blinks. You can't be far away, your silvery voice is close. It floats down these cobbled lanes and thin streets, past the antique shops and cafés and arcades.

Even now, in the car – what used to be my car – you can be heard clearly. Aaron turning the wheel and the vehicle lurching out onto the country road.

'Here.'

I know, but where? I've turned around and there, sitting at the back, is Aaron with Lucy. Look forward and Aaron's handling the wheel to move the car off the road onto gravel, and then grass. 'What's this?'

'You must know, surely. Bernadette showed us where you used to come for a picnic sometimes.'

'I know it damn well is. Bernadette, how could you? This was our secret.'

Someone chuckling. Not laughter though, it's become too high. Now the twittering of a bird high up in the branches.

Why do you have to be like this? Show yourself. I believe you might be hiding on purpose.

'Here – here…'

These infernal trees. Made of stagnant tinsel. They must be covering you. Still I can't see where you are.

Strike the chisel.

34

'Caught up then. Here.' Lucy handing me a sandwich.

Slump to the ground; take it from her. Bitten into it but tastes of sand.

I could do with a drink, I'm parched.

'Here we are.' Bernadette offering, holding out a glass of lager.

I've found you. I'll reach out. How my hand shakes, bruised and battered from the hammer blows missing, grime covering me. Everyone else appears so fresh. Really grateful for this liquid. An appetizing froth on the top; the glass feels cool. Gulp it quickly – pour it into the back of my throat with relish…

I might as well be drinking dust.

Lucy, gazing about. 'Isn't it perfectly lovely.'

Aaron will answer. 'Certainly is. Not many poppies this year.'

I've caught that fond expression appearing on Bernadette's face. He's reaching out. I'm ready to stand up, prepared to defend her.

He's taking a piece of grass from her hair. I should stuff a mouthful of grass down his gullet.

Lucy still giggling. The sea breathes with a rasp.

Bang goes the hammer.

Swollen eyelids, aching numbness; I'm hiding within this flesh which is painful and at the same time without feeling. Can't explain. I'll have to move lumps of plaster from under my aching back, they're digging into me. Yet my back has no sensation of touch.

There's only a gentle covenant of sounds which I can barely perceive, enough to be aware of another existence other than this insulated interior.

How easily I'm able to merge and intertwine realities as easily as balls of string. Here, laying down – in the glade with the burden of sunlight still sapping, washing me away – I can imagine I'm in a darkened room with the lower half of two brick walls, plaster littering the floor, and a disfigured doctor leaking sarcasm from behind.

Have to continue. What's been started must be finished. Almost was lulled into sleep. Must force eyes open, have to find my real Bernadette.

Of course, I'm still here in the woods. Brush away the fly from my cuff. Lucy lying there, outstretched, sucking on a piece of straw, one of her hands waving listlessly.

Bernadette seems to have pulled herself closer to Aaron. I can notice details like this. He's taken off his striped jacket and laid it between us. What does he believe this action symbolizes? They are sitting there, each with the same posture, a mirror of each other, simply looking. Both with lost facial expressions. But eyes can't be disguised. They show a little of one's quintessence. Breathing hard through my nose to attract her attention but still her whole concentration concerns this other man. I have stop myself from lurching forward to pull her to me; to pull her away from him. I detect a slight raising of his left eyebrow. How can I stop them? They're the two halves of one. If only I was able to sever those solid poles of steel connecting them. No, not solid — joined hollow pipes, allowing their locked sights no distraction as they encompass each other, attempt to melt their minds for an illegal spiritual lovemaking.

Over the mountain, watching the watcher...

Must say something to break them apart. 'Looked at Bernadette's palm again, did you?' Swiftly blurted out; tried to accentuate the sarcasm there. Aaron inevitably smiling and nodding. 'A good future has she got? Could you see?' Had to ask to promote a response.

As if time has slowed, he's reaching with a hovering, indecisive hand, to the furred green stem of a dandelion clock.

'Bernadette, must have got your money's worth. In the chalet, I mean. You were there for so long.'

She's poking out the tip of her tongue and it's travelling slowly along her top lip. At the same time, Aaron is holding out the dandelion clock to me with his arm fully extended; bringing the fluffed head to his blank canvas of a face and exhaling through rounded lips, the sound exaggerated, as if made from blowing across the top of a bottle. The lace ball has exploded, white seeds drifting towards where I lay.

How I could scream to perverted memory of Bernadette, 'Stop torturing, giving me this world of pain!' Can't you see how I yearn for the real you, every ounce of myself? There you sit, two feet away, and still we might as well be a thousand miles apart.

See me holding hands up, bloody and blistered. And I'm going to reach out, and at the instance of making contact with your unblemished face, all else will vanish to leave only the two of us, immutable, together for an endlessness of continuation.

What cruelness is this – my hands travelling through you, making you as vague and unreachable as a hallucination, and there behind, I've felt a wall, cold and solid?

'Aaron has such a clever gift.' Sickly admiration. 'You also have glorious healing hands, don't you?'

Do you think I missed that action? Subtle movement of Aaron's index finger towards Lucy, that secret message which Bernadette has obviously interpreted – she nodding back, not as subtly.

I'm going to let out a long breath as though relaxed then close eyes again, an expression of satisfaction about my lips. You'll think I'm unaware of any deviousness though I'm attentive and listening.

A male voice: 'Lucy, are you awake?'

A few bars of birdsong from the woods; the sea a mile away casting onto shingle; my own breathing, husky and unmodulated.

A moment of true silence, before Bernadette breaks it. 'Lucy, wake up.'

'Give her a nudge.'

'Lucy. Lucy.'

A light moan followed by a sniff. 'What's happening? I was miles away then.' I can hear her sitting up.

'What about going for your walk? You said you wanted wild flowers. You ought to go and collect them, now. We'll be making a move soon. What's the time anyway?'

'A quarter to six.'

'If it's that late, I won't bother.'

A tut. 'Yes you will. You particularly wanted flowers, you said. You were most insistent about it. You might want help as well, remember?'

Another pause; Lucy's answering. 'Oh, of course, yeah, right, but he's asleep.'

My leg kicked. Now Bernadette tapping me. 'Donald, Lucy wants to pick some flowers.'

I must give the impression of struggling from sleep. I'll even pretend a yawn. 'Pardon?'

'I said Lucy wants to pick flowers — help her. We haven't got long. We've decided to leave the meal in town and go straight to The Neptune. Get yourself moving.'

'What makes you think I want to pick bloody flowers?'

Lucy has got up, brushing bits from her frock. It's become grass-stained and creased. 'Ready.'

Aaron sitting there looking smug, drinking from a paper cup.

'To help Lucy. It'll be quicker. Don't be a spoilsport.' She can't stop herself from glancing at Aaron, I've noticed.

'I'm sorry but definitely not. Lucy, you might as well sit down again or else pick flowers on your own. I'm not going to pick any. Anyway I don't respond to orders, even yours. Who do you think I am?'

Nobody's answered. Bernadette giving a mean look and as her fingers nip at blades of grass, she's blowing air through her nose. How obvious this is, the devious plot so my wife can be alone with this heinous man.

But I can analyse myself and be aware of a peculiar talent for self-deception. Bernadette is only being difficult. I've probably upset her without realizing. This is her way of retaliating.

There's more, I know, the abandoned filmic hiding just around the corner. Can't quite see this despicable manufactured truth yet I'm beginning to understand there's no way of avoiding it.

35

Take my frustrations out on the wall. I'm going to begin this third one.

Wonder if I dare? My action, under other circumstances, might seem to be unjustified. But I've created a different order. I'm able to develop and refashion new realities. That can't be madness in any form. If anything it should be admired, revered for its excellent inspiration. I will dare and it'll confirm my position in the hierarchy of the greats. I shall be known as a sculptor of time, an accomplished designer of realism.

Choose carefully as if deciding over items in a delicatessen. The bit here: too large. I can afford to be choosy. This piece has embedded brick.

Not fair, just the right size and texture, seeming faultless except it crumbles to powder at the touch.

Better from under the piles instead of picking over silly chips on top. Yes, here we are. First, brush away the loose pieces. Smooth plastered side, the other side uneven as it should be to warrant having. See, doctor? The overall shape is rather interesting – a resemblance to a stone age man's spearhead.

Let it be a pale cheese. Or a sweet white chocolate.

Bitter but I must persevere. I've embarked upon this voyage of discovery; I'll see it through. First bite, small piece at first. There, I've swallowed it, doctor. Easy enough. I'll take a larger piece. I'm salivating like a dog.

Spittle has coated it and again there's no taste. Chewing with confidence. Sort of soft yet crunchy with a sharp, acid flavour, quite unlike chocolate or cheese. The consistency is not what I was expecting.

Rather disheartened. It could have been a useful source of sustenance. Still, I've no time for eating anyway. I've work to finish.

How heavy these implements have become, and how puffed and swollen my fingers are. Feel the rough jolt sear through my blistered palm as the chisel cuts. Lumps pull away from the brickwork, sometimes resentful to part with the mortar beneath.

You still there, doctor? The firm impression I've been talking to myself for the past half hour. You wished me to uncover the last of my barriers; I demand you return.

Won't be bothered by your dancing shadow demons.

I know you've come back now. I feel you leering over my shoulder. Impressed with the progress? Soon it'll be complete.

Though your silence indicates loss of definition. You're slowly fading. It'll not be too long before you'll have lost substance.

You are governed by my laws. As you waver, you can tell me your spirit will survive. But I have to dash your hopes. My rules must be obeyed. Cuckoo souls must not be allowed to roam freely about. Soon you'll have no choice but to join the grand repository of souls, and merge with all others. Quite frankly I'll be glad to see you vanish. Nevertheless, I'm sure to join you there one day. My place is reserved. For the while though, I've urgent work to finish. I have to find the real Bernadette. I keep on losing her; I could almost believe she's trying to avoid me.

36

What an effort to push between these people. The main lights have been turned off and lamps from the discotheque pulse with bright shades in time to the pounding music. Many of the tables have been cleared and chairs and sofas put to the sides. Groups stand chatting and drinking. Pungent cigarette smoke.

I wish I knew where she was. Managed to fight my way to the bar counter. Spotlights from above the bar form a bright block in this flashing room – it's a floating lighted island. I'll peer along the length of the bar. A mass of individuals lining it with more standing behind. Lucky to have got this place quickly. There are extra bar staff to cope with the increase in the number of customers and they move from the bar to the optics and hand pumps, deftly avoiding each other in a practiced way, weaving about in an energetic fashion.

Four heads away, the one with the ten pound note in his hand: I recognize him. One of Aaron's friends. I was reluctantly introduced to him earlier. I'll attempt to make my way around, perhaps he can help.

Pushing through here, squeezing by there, excuse me while I hit the chisel…

Why won't he turn? I've tapped him twice on the shoulder. Mercifully, music has stopped for a short while. I really couldn't cope with it, being so loud, loud, loud, being so unfortunately tired. I'll have to tap him once more.

He's spun around. 'What? What is it?'

'Have you seen my wife?' My voice is timid. Throat inflamed and raw. If only I had time to buy a drink but I must find Bernadette.

Bawling his reply. 'Is that all? Can't you see I'm trying to get my pint? Wait a minute.' Several party guests about him have turned their attention to me, grinning as though I've told a joke.

The pulsing music has started again, sending sympathetic waves pounding through me. Those lights are flashing red, yellow, blue, orange, green – tainting these happy revellers. Women are dancing over by the double doors, throwing their heads back, and waving their limbs while they twist and gyrate. A couple of youths – I recognize them as the fountain guardians – stand by the large figurehead. See one then, impertinently stroking his wooden beard.

For an instant I thought I saw Aaron over by the panelled wall but it's someone else wearing a striped jacket.

Wield the hammer, smack on the chisel.

Aaron's friend is having to bellow over the music. 'What did you say?' He's shouted so loudly in my ear, it's stung it.

I'll shout in return. 'I asked if you've seen my wife. She's around somewhere. Wondered if you've spotted her.'

He's draining beer from a glass jug. How I could do with a drink. My fingers are fiddling nervously with the hair on the back of this wig. Taken them away and such a cloud of white dust produced. He's not seeming to notice. I'll have to pull back to read the reply from his lips. An age before he responds. The flashing lights are changing his expressions. The red makes him appear brutal and impatient but then as the lights become yellow, his features are made softer, and acquire a forlorn appearance. He's taking the last gulp of beer.

With this pale blue upon him his visage has transformed again. Can you see it as clearly as I can? It's become sarcastic and contemptuous. He yells with each word living in its own colour: 'How the fuck should I know?' Those broad shoulders shrugging as he turns orange and walks away, disappearing into the throng about the bar.

Everybody is flashing teeth in pristine clothing, laughing and dancing, holding each other as well as their drinks, none with a care. But my worries have dragged me down, covered me with apathy and concern.

Merciless music pauses again. I'll make my way over to the doors leading to the beer garden. Maybe she's gone outside.

I can see the fountain through the doorway.

Those about the slatted tables and picnic benches are enjoying the summer evening. Couples strolling by, arm in arm, lit by the rows of lanterns strung between the trees. The sounds of water lapping the seawall and the waves breaking on the beach further along might have been, on another evening, soothing and romantic, but tonight I've no time for it. I must find my wife. Scan the garden again. To the left, sitting close together on the bench, hidden in shadow – can't be certain but...

Strike the chisel, techno drum blows to the wall.

Barring my way: this girl blocking me from advancing further. In fact, I'm forced to step back into the panelled room with its clamour and mad lights as she leans towards me in an intimate fashion. Can't she see I'll make her frock dirty? Anyway, I've no desire to stimulate any sort of relationship with this young lady. I've love for one woman only. And I'm desperate to find her.

Lucy slurring. 'If it isn't diddly Donald. Fancy meeting you here. Buy my drink now? Vodka and orange. Don't forget the cherry and the tiny twirly umbrella.' Why she has to push her breasts forward like that I really don't know. It's obviously unnatural. Noticed she's not wearing a bra. Her lipstick has been smeared. 'And then how about a romantic smooch?' Her hand has snaked about my waist. I'll have to remove it.

'Sorry but no. I want to find Bernadette. You have seen her, haven't you? She's out there, isn't she?' I must try to push past but she won't let me. I can't be too emphatic in my actions otherwise I would be seen by these other party guests.

Her reply slow with delight. 'Yup, I know where.' A girl

dancing between us, her arms waving like seaweed fronds. 'And,' Lucy continuing in a sing-song voice, 'I know what she's up to.'

'What do you mean?' They are there, out on the bench by the hotel wall in the hulking shadows, next to each other, maybe contemplating the scene, nothing more. 'Excuse me please, Lucy. I insist you let me pass.'

Fluttering her eyelashes in such an affected way. 'You don't want to leave, silly man. Dance the night away. I bet you're secretly a good mover. Show me.'

Yet again she's hauling me, this time away from the doors. The red and yellow and orange and blue man is closing them.

On the bench outside, they're conversing…

'Donald, here, dance with me, forget out there. They'll be alright. They're having a long, hard, big, chat.'

Next to each other but then his arm has found its way about her shoulders…

'Move your hips more, like this; yeah, better—'

Those beats of music are jarring, still keeping time with blows to the chisel until perhaps he's placed himself closer…

'You understand I'm pulling you to the bar? Sneaky aren't I.' Yelled in my ear. 'Going to buy me this flippin' drink?'

Damn it, I've hit my finger again. Begun to bleed. At the same time, instantaneously, this striking has signalled him moving his lips to hers, tongue pushing into her mouth, her hands in his hair while his are massaging her breasts; a sudden ravaging, trying to get as close together as possible, salivating in their passion, not caring who else might see this display in the shadowy murkiness; letting out small utterances, enjoying until wanting to abuse each other; for in the throes of desire one can forget the other which has become the you, and You must feed You, and feed on you, a selfish mastication until sated but you can never be filled, and demand more and get more, and more…

Won't take any more of this, I have to push Lucy away. So insidiously leech-like she's become, there's the tearing release of suction. I'll force her down to the ground. I don't care for her. She's in league with the others. And they have formed ranks before the double doors like a battalion line of soldiers.

This is a dungeon delusion or else I'm going politely insane.

There must be a weapon here somewhere. I have to get to my wife before it's too late. The stuffed fox has limped from the protection of its coat stand and is weaving in and out between my legs in a figure of eight, no doubt trying to bewilder me. On the wall at the back, surrounded by oil lamps and photographs, is one of the long glass-fronted cases. That'll do. I feel low, unwashed and somewhat slightly dazed; I'm bringing the hammer high to reach it. I'll strike the case – the glass has shattered. Someone shrieked at the breaking glass and it's too obvious in the room: the music has stopped again. I'll reach up to snatch the narwhal horn from the case and grip it to my side, the twisted rod ready to threaten those who would try to stop me. Must have cut my palms on the glass shards because they're bloody and slipping on it. Everyone is shocked or frightened by my actions. And so they should be; they must understand how determined I am. I wish them no harm but I will charge those by the doors if necessary. But look, there's no need. I was certain if I menaced them they would see reason. All but one has stepped aside. This last person has opened the doors, ushering me through with a sweep of an arm and a generous bow. And if it wasn't for that sneer I'd think he was a type of servant.

At last I'm in the garden.

37

Bernadette has unlocked from her embrace – tears springing readily from her – now running into the bar. Aaron has his hands high with his palms towards me as though the point of the narwhal bone near his heart was a gun.

'Don't do anything you might regret.'

How ill at ease he sounds!

'Move over there.' I've indicated with the long bone which is aggravating my blistered and bleeding hands. But I can't let go, for the power which I've gained would leave me as surely as water spinning from a bathtub. This vigorous force is instilled in the horn or hammer, whichever I have here. Unable to tell. It doesn't matter, either one is vibrating with a robust potency. Finally, I'm able to destroy this person who has brought me so much misery. He's sniggering but I know it's a nervous reaction to cover his fright. I'm making him walk backwards through the massive bleached arched bones of a whale. As he comes upon chairs or tables, other guests are moving them out of the way. I can control them all, you see.

Everyone is feeling my omnipotence, tasting my power. Go on, further, you miserable dog, smarmy snake, though careful not to trip. Like that but luckily you've not fallen but continue, staggering backwards to the railings. Gulls in this night sky like white ash floating from a bonfire. They're silent for a change, aware of what is about to happen, knowing of this reconstructed past future.

'You can't do this. No harm meant, of course. Forgive me, Donadette, and I'll repair the situation. I'm deeply ashamed of my actions; never in my wildest dreams wished to harm your feelings. Believe me, I want to repay you if you'll allow it, help heal the damage caused. Will you let me do that much? Can I? Can we be friends? Do you see my sorrow?'

No, frankly I don't.

Again duality of action, balance of twoness: as I clout the metal, biting into the forgiving plaster, so the long weapon, javelin-like, is thrown into the night.

I wish to savour this.

I'm able to slow it down as if it were on film and watch my missile toned by the Chinese lanterns in shimmering shades. See it describe a precise semi-circle as graceful to observe as a diver plunging between Castor and Pollux until my elegant projectile punctures his body. It's made a sound like plaster falling from a wall.

I could create a theatrical howl of agony from him, and have a slopping rope of blood come where he's been struck, as well as where it's left the body in the small of his back. But no, I'll merely have this skewered man close his evil eyes to the beer garden and on the life he's to leave. And if there's to be a stream emitting, I would want it to be his life-force seeking sanctuary in the very place from where it came from. There he goes, losing balance as vitality betrays him and leaves a sinking ship. He's falling over the railings into the murky sea below. Not much of a splash. He's slipped silently under.

I observe that the jetty beer garden has returned to normal. Youngsters with their cans of fizz chasing each other with excited squeals, adults busy drinking, trying to forget work and their pressing concerns.

Smoke and hubbub in the bar hits me, and your voice. You've shouted so loudly it's hurt my eardrum. Really wish I could be free from you.

'I think you're deaf, you know. I asked for my drinky.'

'I will, Lucy, but first I've got to find her. She has to be here somewhere. It's as though she's hiding, trying to avoid me.' But there, next to me. Why I didn't see you before, I really don't know. 'Where have you been? I was fretting.'

'Don't be stupid, Donald. Lucy, this is Frank, another of Aaron's friends. Have you bumped into Aaron?'

Bernadette has put her back to me. Is it because I'm dirty with muck, and need a shave and a bath, need to repair the homage makeup and torn skirt? I can understand that. She has her arm linked with Frank's. I want to pull her away.

I'll take her hand in mine.

For a second I'm within an empty space with the bottom halves of its walls deprived of plaster, and Bernadette squeezing my knuckles tightly, blisters hurting. But no more quickly – the loud bar jammed with its crowd has returned. She's snatched her hand from mine as if I've burned her. I'll take hold of it once more but she pulls it away again, complaining between clenched teeth. 'Don't be so damned pathetic.' Lucy and Frank are smirking. 'Nobody else holds hands. If you want to do that then hold your own.'

'There, there,' interrupts Lucy. She's slithered up to my side. 'I'll hold your hand, Donald.'

My wife finding it amusing. I must try to speak again but the dust in my throat is preventing me.

'Anyway,' Lucy informs us, 'Aaron was over by the bar, five minutes ago.' Grinning, to me. 'After he'd finished his sexy dance with I wonder who. Know what I mean?'

Couldn't fail to notice the sharp jab Lucy received in the ribs. And to underline the message, Bernadette saying, 'Shut up, Lucy.' She's turned to me. 'Donald, get some drinks.'

'Oh, you've decided it's my round, I see. Another order, is it? As it happens I don't want a drink. I want a dance. I feel energies returning.'

'I've got to find Aaron, for Frank.'

The guy hasn't been paying much attention. He's wandered away; now chatting to someone by the engravings.

She's trying to antagonize me. I've hardly the strength but dancing is a way to be close to her. 'Why can't you do something I want for a change? I'm convinced real Bernadette is hiding in you. I might get drinks later.' I could happily buy a drink but I'll not let her doppelgänger win this time.

Her hands are on her hips. One of her favourite stances lately. The possibilities of an argument, especially in public, is beginning to arouse her. But before she can speak, Lucy speaks. 'I'll dance with Mr Donald Duck – we'll bop the night away,' and before I can reply she's leading me over to where several couples move gently to slow music. She's plastered herself to me. And in the time it takes to revolve a full, annoyingly slow, three hundred and sixty degrees about this noisy, bustling room with its coloured lights, my wife has disappeared again.

Doctor, this is becoming another bad dream. My every move is frustrated. Mercifully the beat is gentle and I can match the pace when lifting the hammer. It's grown to weigh ten times more than when I started.

Lucy rocking me and whispering. I'm finding it most irritating. Burying her face into my filthy blouse. Surprised she hasn't sneezed.

'Where's she gone this time? Lucy, you must help.'

Ignoring me and I'm snarling. This snarl, doctor, like this?

We're revolving faster. The ridiculous music is speeding up, I'm convinced. The bass drum is the pump pulse of my enraged heart. With a particularly nimble expertise, Lucy is manoeuvring me about the floor and between the others as if I were a dodgem. Now and then she anticipates incorrectly and I'm steered into a couple, or collide with a table. Each time this happens, watch the white fog come from me.

I'm unable to control this situation. Becoming dominant and overtaking.

Difficult to see faces with shadow and these infuriating lights, but also the speed we're turning. The exercise is debilitating. The pace is becoming too much. How can I repel a girl who has a supernatural grip?

Faster and faster we rotate, the thumping pulses matching us. Is the music keeping with our speed or is it the other way around? Let me rest.

Dizzily spinning we are, a crazy roundabout. This erratic, mad twirling sending me flying uncontrollably about as empty and lifeless as a deflated balloon. The whole of my body hollow, all there sapped. Bile in my throat making me wretch. Two-inch nail driven between my eyebrows.

And now the oddness, both of being and of knowing…

I'm able to be in several places at the same time. See me revolving on an axis, sent about and around like a wild tornado. Then the see is the I see, for I view myself; watching me – in a tangerine dream – perhaps from a corner by the stuffed carp with starfish placed about it like asterisks; or the I adhered to the wall above the door lintel as though a fly or spider — then at the attempt to define the startled insect form, I understand I'm a moth. And there's a third me, on the floor of a small office littered with broken plaster. And this variant could easily lay down to sleep, or die. Not sure of the difference at the moment nor really care.

My sore eyes. They've been prised from their sockets and empty bone bowls filled with grit before being pushed back in.

I'll lick my hands like a dog. The stinging is constant.

But know this: send me more pain and sorrow or lurid torment – any mixture of these – or curdling distress in its murkiest form. Whatever's decided, I will cope. I'll not go under. I must endure for the survival of my consciousness to be guaranteed, to find the real her. Or at least for as long as it takes to finish this important job. This is the hard school I must learn. Bring me any type of trauma on its dull slab and I'll transform it – the shapeless shoddiness of it – into something manageable and uplifted.

Oddly enough it's none of these holding fear for me. The one which can induce utter panic is the stealthy one, the soft, plumping-pillow one which is marshmallowing me away. And it mustn't be given the chance to take hold. Take up thy tools and work. Put the chisel to the wall and then angle it for the best purchase for when metal strikes metal.

Not the metallic ring as expected but the music rudely interrupting again. Surprisingly its insistent beat can bring me a renewed strength to slow the uncontrollable spin to a standstill. Lucy still in my grip. You know where the real Bernadette is. How many more times do I ask? Where? Where? Where?

She seeming perplexed. 'Steady on, Donny. You've had one too many. There she is.'

38

Passing in front of me, pressed to Aaron, she is there – and if only I had another five seconds before they were swamped by other couples, I might have been certain she was kissing his neck.

No Lucy, do release me. You're as many-limbed as an octopus. I have to speak to her. There's an urgency. Not too long before this last wall's ready. I still might be able to alter the outcome.

See the trail of seaweed where they've been. And when I come upon them I understand why. Aaron has a decaying stench about him with barnacles covering his hands and face. The texture of any skin not covered has desiccated and become striated like bark. The eyes have gone, leaving bleak holes as impenetrably black as moonless night. He speaks and from between those puce, swollen lips gushes spurts of tiny fishes. 'Agreed then. I'll put you up for the night.' My wife is giggling rudely.

I'm not sure what he means or really what's happening.

Surely this foul man should be dead. I can see the stump of the narwhal bone covered in slime, protruding from his chest.

'Bernadette, let's go. I've had enough. I'm desperate for sleep but not yet. The last wall isn't quite finished. Anyhow it's time we went home, time we started from square one.'

Lucy remarking: 'Time you were tucked up with your hot water bottle.'

'Aaron is offering to put us up. He's got a spare bed. No need to be unreasonable, Donald. You've had a few drinks. And it's unfair to ask Aaron to drive us home. He only lives a few roads away.'

This is a conspiracy made behind my back. 'I want to sleep in my own bed.'

Bernadette's soul thief smirk. 'Fair enough. See you tomorrow.'

'What's that meant to mean?'

'A joke, Donald. Just look at yourself. As usual you're being perfectly unreasonable. There's no alternative. It's not friendly to refuse an invitation.'

'You've both worked this out. No alternative you say. Haven't you heard of taxis? And surely, Aaron, you can't be upset just because we want to get home.'

His laugh is really ugly. A gurgling from the back of his throat. His breath is fetid. Making me want to retch. I've become as weak as a kitten. How clever they've become. The tables have turned again as swiftly as in a chess tournament. It's quite knocked me off balance. I'm unable to control destiny. My power must have left me with the release of the bone from the narwhal. Confusion muddling my reasoning; a measured panic has me again. My heartbeats are tripping over. I don't know where I am. Is this the bar of The Neptune Hotel? It should be, I was here a few minutes ago. But it's changed. There's only the four of us. The bar staff have vanished. Something very peculiar is happening; it's unreal. Without my noticing, the maritime items have been taken from the ceiling and it's empty, except for that large circular lamp stuck there. More peculiar are the walls. Panelling and the pictures have gone and the plaster removed. My three companions don't seem worried by this. Perhaps I should calm down. There's a vague memory for I've a dusted-white hammer and a chisel in my hands. But why would I want to take plaster from the walls of The Neptune Hotel? Illogical. It should not be.

On with the show: these tools must go.

The instant they were thrown to the floor: the walls are better covered in wallpaper, and the settee and the carpet are an improvement on the cold marble tables and wrought iron chairs. The double doors have been covered with patterned curtains. My wife is filling my glass again with red wine. I'm painfully dry mouthed, doctor. I can barely keep away sleep. The glass must go back to a coffee table before the liquid is spilt. This task is more than I'm capable of. Thankfully I can feel it taken from my burning hand.

A moment of true silence.

Every ounce of me will be still until the tranquillity is broken.

'Time we were off to bed.' Have I dribbled this? If given a choice I would have remained silent.

'You know what that means don't you?' A crude laugh.

My breathing is sounding shallow. This terrible veil between me and all else. A unique experience, this final debilitation.

I'm still yearning for you, Bernadette. I need to hold you close, let your perfume overpower the filth, have your bewitching form become a blockade against the ugliness and dirtiness I feel. I know you're there, though I've no means of contact. I'm aware of being crushed.

Definitely someone else's voice. At least, it's coming from outside.

'Drunken slob, look at him. Hope he doesn't spew on your settee. Do you think we put too much powder in his drink? Give me a hand will you, Aaron? Get him upstairs out of the way. You're going as well aren't you, Lucy.'

I sense these last words are a demanding statement more than a question although I'll expect a reply.

Spin, spin, spin…

There's a click, a suspiration, then a rustling, then a chink and a rattle, then another voice speaking. The words are undefined yet can still be understood when I'm pulled up from the settee, my head lolling uselessly. I'm not sure how many times these same words are spoken as an answer. Already I've listened to them innumerable times. So full of intent do these three words possess, they're able to replicate and multiply; so filled with insinuation and potential they can feed me a spoonful of energy for my eyelids to open as I'm helped with rough, uncaring hands upstairs; a banister rail spinning one way with Lucy holding on tight, her fists white as she spins the other way, uttering her triplet of words just once more.

'I suppose so.'

39

As the final piece of plaster was cleaved from the base of the fourth wall, a distant police siren warbled into the night. Then, but for the monotonous ticking of the clock and its occasional whirring as if taking a breath, it could have been as though everyone but Clement had ceased to exist. A fine suspension of dust hung in a ghostly fashion within a glow produced from the foyer lamps, this light diluted and modified by the sheets of newspaper taped across the pane of the reception office. A pencil beam of brightness – as relatively bright as a laser – came from a horizontal slit which had escaped from being covered. For an instant, Clement believed he hadn't left the interior of his wardrobe and that if he were to push firmly onto the top of the string of light, a door would swing outward and once more would he fall – this time defying gravity and falling upwards – out onto his rug. But of course, he told himself firmly, this would be preposterous. Wherever I am, it's certainly not in my wardrobe cocoon.

He lay still, exhausted and dazed on piles of plaster, as limp as any dead man. Dust plugged his nostrils and coated his parched throat, and he wheezed with every irregular breath. The wig had turned white. His vivacious makeup was smeared and had become pastel shades. Blood had dried brown and streaked his knuckles.

As the timer in the cupboard switched the lights off in the foyer, the yellow-painted door appeared phosphorescent in the twilight of the reception office. It stood starkly against the rough, ruby wine-coloured bricks. Clement's sight rested upon the door and immediately it appeared to take a step back – even lean away – intimating it would never open again.

40

Going blind I'm almost certain. There's a leaden dusk within this strange room. But how much of the obscurity is due to negative lighting or my eyeballs boiling I really don't know. Other senses are deserting though I can't blame them as I've renounced the outside world of pretence. It's as though all has been cloaked, washed with black. No longer can I smell or taste. Mouth and nose must surely be stuffed with wadding. Help, I can't breathe properly. Wheezing like an old buffalo. Unable to hear well. Hands are useless. Is it you who's pushed needles under the skin and nails, Dr Leibkov? I'm losing control. If only the padding would come out – here, with my fingers down my throat – I'm gagging but all that's ejected is bursts of noxious gas. I can't sense and it's a handicap as I fight against an insubstantial enemy, as though locked in massive combat, grappling a thick medium, heaving, sweating.

Who is this enemy? If it has a grip on me then it also has hold over somebody else. There's weeping.

The outside has finally become one with my inside. No

visible or definable areas to say where one ends and the other begins.

Time to turn, and turn, and turn again.

I have absorbed everything.

Animal and vegetable life are mine sheltered within; this domain I've become teems with trillions of insects; microbes and viruses have found their haven here, and spaces between filled with every atom stocked with quarks and larks and farks and all else.

To encompass so much I must have taken in the planet and its orbit. It can't be long before I harbour the known universe of galaxies until I am one.

After that I'll have to wrap myself in cotton wool. I need to be protected with glass fibre or metals, be tough, impenetrable, opaque. Cocooned by red thoughts, become as isolated and untouched as a deserted island in a vast ocean.

Then I wouldn't have to listen – I recognize the sounds of a woman's tormented voice.

Doctor, doctor, this is all of your doing. You are banished. I'll never see or hear of your complicated falsehoods again.

Life is but a dream.

There are gasps of pain interspersed with racking whines. What's happening? I must stop this torture.

Again I'm disoriented. Struggling to release myself from sheets which have bound me within a sarcophagus of a bed.

Not enough light to see. I've kicked a wall — aah, the pain jolting up my leg. As I cried out though, my utterance drowned by agonizing sobs coming from somewhere in this house. A noise of something tipped over.

I have to stop this. Difficult to locate the door handle. A long groan emitted, low in pitch.

The door's open and I'm on a landing.

What manner of cruel instruments are being used on this woman? The tormentor shouting in guttural barks and her voice raised higher in coughing bursts. My shadow, made by an electric lamp from down there, has decided to trail to my side while I pad down these stairs. I wish I knew where I was. Can't be my house because my staircase has no carpet.

The walls are of brick only, there's no plaster on them. I'm going to float downwards. My legs have no feeling while I curl up in this manner. I've become as a migrating chrysalis. I must await renewal which surely will be mine once I'm ready. It's growth, change, maturation to fruition until decay begins. For then debris of death incorporates the components of a new life to develop from.

I must admit suffering to reach my goal of rebirth.

First though, the matter in hand. I have to solve one last puzzle of the dream, the riddle of the sensibilities, before I can let go to my inevitable destiny. The woman's cries of agony. I've no more idea of her identity than a meaning of life until, in wrought pulses, she's panting, 'Yes…'

No, it has come to me, this is my wife crying out; she's crying, crying out — and I hurry down the stairs, like an encumbered wraith, like I was not really there, like my bound body existed somewhere else.

And I float on the ceiling and stare down.

And what is and what should never be: the narwhal bone has hit me full between the eyebrows to split open my head. And with a ripping, my skull has parted into two, as wide as those woman's legs straddled over the man on his back, belonging to yet another girl who's stolen my wife's face. And who is this laying beneath her, panting and grumbling obscenities, the lower torso pumping up and down in that manner, stinking of slippery seaweed and covered with barnacles, though I suspect it could be Dr. Leibkov.

And in their energetic motion they're both vocalizing filth in ambition of climactic moment, unaware of my presence in some form or other.

And I must quickly become blind again as my soul is torn apart and bleeding, cover writhing nakedness with barricades and barriers, build a fortress over them.

And this beginning is the end, the end to be the beginning. Jagged gothic horizon.

Capturing visions of future, I know how I'll be reborn: in a form as venerated as any king might deserve who rules his land, who's majesty is in command; to be an honourable and graceful existence blessed with serenity and balance, and oneness of twoness, and perfect infinity and stillness.

Not a chrysalis — I'm a seed. Return to nought of the web of time.

I'm becoming a tree, newly risen. It makes sense if world is within. It's a turning inside out again. Bury roots into lush earth. And here I'll stay, stable and unchanging, never moving or being moved – no visions of angels – unsullied by emotion or event. Able to do nothing except exist so that the passage of time will pass unchallenged and without interaction. And if one human sensibility is allowed, it should be patience in silence, in preparation for the other side of my soul; to wait for my real, beautiful Bernadette who'll come to me with the happiest of laughs and pure love in her heart, and who will gladly throw her arms about me to set me free.

DAVID JOHN GRIFFIN is a writer, graphic designer and app designer, and lives in a small town by the Thames in Kent, UK with his wife Susan and two dogs called Bullseye and Jimbo. He is currently working on the first draft of a third novel as well as writing short stories for a forthcoming collection.

His first novel, The Unusual Possession of Alastair Stubb, was published by Urbane in November 2015. Urbane will also publish David's magical realism/paranormal novella, Two Dogs At The One Dog Inn, in the spring of 2017. One of his short stories was shortlisted for The HG Wells Short Story competition 2012 and published in an anthology.

You can find out more about David at
www.davidjohngriffin.com

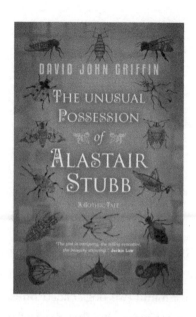

"Dark and at times shocking the book contains some lovely writing and has a great gothic feel to it. I can recommend this to you and it's well worth a read if unusual is what you require."

DAVID REVIEWS (Amazon Top 500 Reviewer)

"Here's a virtual round of applause for the author, who has created an amazingly surreal world where devilry thrives – it's a hauntingly good read."

LITTLE BOOKNESS LANE

The turn of the last century and Theodore Stubb's manor house resides in the quirky village of Muchmarsh. A renowned entomologist, he is often within the attic adding another exotic specimen to his extensive collection of insects. But Theodore is also a master hypnotist, holding the household in thrall to his every whim.

Theodore's daughter-in-law Eleanor − returned from the sanatorium two months before − is a haunted figure, believing that her stillborn child Alastair lives and hides in the shadows. Then she falls pregnant again, but this time by the hypnotic coercion and wicked ravishment of Theodore. A dreadful act begets terrible secrets, and thirteen years later the boy Alastair Stubb begins to lose his identity….it is not long before mystery, intrigue and murder follow gleefully in his wake.

The Unusual Possession of Alastair Stubb is a gothic terror of the highest order, delivering a dream-like and hallucinatory reading experience that promises to reveal secrets both disturbing and astonishing. Do you dare meet the Stubbs?

£8.99, ISBN 978-1-910692-45-5

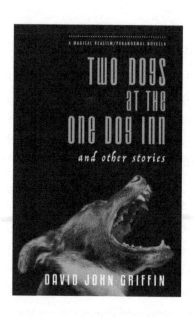

"*This novella is uniquely written, the mysterious plot is revealed through a series of email conversations between two characters. The story line keeps you intrigued throughout, Highly recommended.*"

PETER DRAPER

"*I read this novella in one day, as I was intrigued with the story. It was at times unnerving, a tale of fantasy and love, and very entertaining. The author has a very vivid and wild imagination. He described the scenes so well, I could picture, taste, and feel everything before me. It's written via a series of emails between Stella and Audrey, plus diary entries. It was a most enjoyable read!*"

H.M. MARTIN

The novella: Dogs are reported for their constant barking ... and so begins one of the strangest stories you will ever read.

Audrey Ackerman, sent to visit the dogs at a 17th century coach house, is unsettled by paranormal sightings.

Stella Bridgeport – manager at The Animal Welfare Union – communicates with Audrey via emails. And those Stella receives are as startling as they are incredible: descriptions of extraordinary events concerning a science fiction writer's journal; giant swans; bizarre android receptionist; a ghost dog.

Insanity or fantasy? Fact or fiction? The only given is, it all starts and ends with two dogs at The One Dog Inn.

...and other stories: 12 short stories with aspects of the macabre, the surreal, science fiction or the strangeness of magical realism to entertain and delight you.

£8.99, PAPERBACK

AVAILABLE ON AMAZON AND IN ALL GOOD
BOOKSHOPS from March 2017 onwards